THE DISAPPEARING DOG DILEMMA

The Gabby St. Claire Diaries, Book 2

By Christy Barritt
and Kathy Applebee

Published by River Heights

Cover design by The Killion Group

Kathy Applebee would like to thank:

Christy Barritt, who continues to encourage and prune me while allowing me and my imaginary friends into Gabby's world.

Mary Penuel, a friend who sticks closer than a brother through thick and thin.

My husband Michael, his pet sitting business provided inspiration and his daily sacrifices allowed me the opportunity to pursue a dream. I love you.

My Creator, who watches over sparrows, me and the entire world. May He be magnified forever.

Christy Barritt would like to thank:

My kids, who bring so much joy into my life.

CHAPTER 1

Pet sitting was not turning out to be an easy-peasy, fun job after all. First, when my mom had said each visit would take thirty minutes tops, she hadn't factored in travel time. Even in our old van with the back bumper held on by duct tape, the trip to the Wrangleys' was less than five minutes. In the wintry air with the sun going down, walking seemed to take half a day, not half an hour. By the time I arrived, I was a shuffling iceberg complete with a drippy nose and numb fingers and toes.

I jammed the key into the lock so hard my hand slipped and smacked into the side of the door.

Ouch! Even with frozen fingers, the pain made me suck on my bruised knuckle. I tried again, more carefully, wondering why Pocococo wasn't scratching at the door and whining. That was his typical modus operandi (that's detective talk for usual behavior). He had been dying to see me this morning, which was the second downside to pet sitting: no matter how cute the dog, no thirteen-year-old in their right mind feels like playing at 6:00 a.m. Don't get me wrong, Pocococo is the cutest Chihuahua this side of Mexico, but if the sun's not up, I shouldn't be either.

But he should be at the door at dinnertime.

Another gust of wind whipped my frizzy, shoulder-length hair into my eyes and below my nose, and I wished for the gazillionth time I had a tissue in my pocket. As I pushed open the door, a horrible thought crossed my mind, chilling it like the wind had my body.

Not another disappearing dog! Three other canines had been stolen from Oceanside Veterinary Clinic and Boarding last weekend. It was the only reason I had this paying gig; the owners were afraid to leave him at a doggy hotel. Only the promise of extra cash could motivate me to trek through the tundra of Virginia Beach.

I bet nobody mentions the Arctic windblasts of March in the tourist brochures.

I threw the door open and dashed inside, delighted to feel the warmth curl around me. I imagined I was a piece of bread in a toaster. Heavenly bliss! My elation was short lived. My heart started pounding as I became aware of the danger smack dab in front of me in the den.

A homeless man was lounging on the couch, scratching Pocococo's ears. I recoiled involuntarily, my brain trying to make sense of what my eyes were seeing.

No one should be here – especially not this bum! I have to escape!

My backward motion sent one foot sliding on the throw rug that lay bunched from when I opened the door. I tried to catch my balance, tried to grab something, but my frozen fingers found nothing but thin air. My numb toes were flying out from under me.

Thump!

I landed hard on the doormat on the porch, skinning an elbow. I scrabbled to get up, trying desperately to decide what to do. I was torn between lingering ever so briefly to shut the door and keep Pocococo from escaping, and just running for my life. My indecisiveness cost me. Pocococo was out the door in a flash.

I ran as fast as my short legs would carry me, both to catch Pocococo and to flee from the unexpected stranger. I had to remember what he looked like so I could tell the police.

Long, dark hair, unkempt. Scruffy, dark

beard. Army-green jacket and dirty jean cutoffs. Bandaged foot and leg on a pillow.

Whoa! Bandaged foot?

I slowed and whirled. No one was chasing after me, and for good reason. The man was a cripple or hurt or maybe just really, really ancient.

The sound of an approaching car interrupted my agitated train of thought. Pocococo was prancing in the road, oblivious that he was directly in the path of the oncoming car. I waved and shouted to get the driver's attention as I sprinted down the middle of the street. I scooped up the excited little dog. The annoyed driver honked as he barely slowed down, forcing me to leap to the curb opposite the Wrangleys' house.

"Ever heard of a leash law?" snarled the driver. He punched the accelerator and sped away.

Pocococo began licking my hands and wiggling. The Chihuahua gave a couple of sharp barks and tried to climb up my jacket to wash my face.

"Shush!" I coaxed. I surveyed both sides of the street for someone, anyone. I needed to call the police and report the break-in. I thought about flagging down a car, but the only one in sight carried the irritated driver down the street at least ten over the speed limit.

My heart was still beating hard, but the initial shock of the strange man, escaped dog, and homicidal driver was wearing off.

"We're just going to have to get to the corner store and have them place a 911 call," I confided to the dog and broke into a jog.

"Hey, I'll call the cops if you try to dognap Pocococo," shouted a rough voice behind me.

Still jogging, I spared a backward glance.

"With that red hair you'll be easy to pick out of a lineup," the bum continued.

He knows Pocococo's name! How?

I stopped, turned, and demanded, "Who are you and how did you get in? How do you know this is Pocococo?" I cradled the little guy protectively in my arms.

It finally registered that Pocococo had been sitting on the man's lap, but I wasn't taking any chances. This bum couldn't possibly be legit. The Wrangleys would have mentioned him. My mind considered a flurry of possibilities.

He'd broken in because of the cold. Or he'd escaped from a military mental hospital on the neighboring Oceana naval air base. Or he was one of the dognappers who'd been casing the Wrangleys' place for the last couple days to steal Pocococo.

"I could ask you the same thing." The man leaned on a cane and stood awkwardly in the doorway.

I noticed he wasn't really, really old, just kind of old. Like maybe thirty or something.

"I happen to be the pet sitter, that's who. And I have a key." As soon as the words left my mouth, I realized I didn't have the key. It, along with my flip-flop key ring and my own house key, was still dangling on the other side of the door.

I had to get those keys. Otherwise, he might notice them, find my family's duplex, and . . .

I swallowed. I started to perspire and, since the March weather was still lionlike, I knew it was fear that pulled the moisture from my body. A gust of the wind tugged at my hair. Pocococo whined and tried to claw his way out of my grip.

What should I do? Was the intruder linked to the three other missing dogs? Why did I ever take this job?

I could answer the last question. It had all started Monday at lunch.

CHAPTER 2

I could hear and smell the Oceanside Middle School cafeteria forty feet away. Greasy fries, old cardboard boxes, and the noise of 150 seventh graders crammed into a chow hall built for economy of space, not separation of cliques, leaked into the seventh-grade hallway. Posters of cartoon fruits and veggies covered water stains and cracked paint, but who cared? My peepers would be focused on Brandon, the most gorgeous green-eyed guy in the universe.

I still found it hard to believe he ate at my table five days a week. Technically, it wasn't my private little table for two or anything, because my BFF Becca, Pete, and Paulette sat there too. But it was Brandon that could send me into a Brance (my own private word for the trance Bran the Man put me into at least fifty-five billion times a day).

I, Gabby St. Claire, had a crush.

Brandon Coe was the coolest, the hottest, and

the warmest. That may sound like a contradiction in terms, but it isn't. I figured he was like light, because light could be both a particle and a wave at the same time. And Bran was the light of my life.

Of course, there were a couple of complications. Just teensy-weensy ones, starting with the fact that he was already taken by Pete's older sister, Lana. There was also the minor detail that my best friend had a major crush on him, too. So, at the moment, I worshipped him from afar and sat next to him at lunch.

Because I always brought my lunch, I bypassed the lunch line and headed straight to the middle section of the cafeteria, where three ten-foot-long tables shoved together like a barricade divided the out and in crowds. Officially, we didn't have assigned seats, but unofficially we did. It was the middle-school equivalent of a felony to infringe on another clique's territory.

I dropped into a seat and stared out the window at the wintry downpour outside. Snow and therefore snow days were rare in Virginia Beach. Too bad school administrators didn't close school for cold, dreary, freezing rain. I knew we needed it, but why couldn't precipitation schedule itself to fall between 2:00 and 4:00 a.m. when I was sound asleep?

Outside, a drab gray car belched a slight figure onto the dirty gray pavement in front of our aging school. The figure dashed for the door, backpack hoisted above her head to protect her orange hair from the drizzle dropping from the steel-gray clouds.

My BFFLs (best friends for lunch) weaved through the crazed masses to reach our oasis of sanity as Becca listened intently to the gorgeous but unavailable Brandon. No surprises there. He could recite the Pledge of Allegiance, and Becca would hang on every word.

Becca's pixie nose and haircut were at odds with her long arms and legs. She took her seat across from me, just a little closer to Brandon on her right than she needed to be.

"Hey, guys. What's shaking?" I asked.

Brandon turned his dazzling green eyes to mine. Even after two months, his gaze could start a flush crawling up my neck and across my face. I quickly broke eye contact to look at something safer. I turned to study Pete, who picked at his mac and cheese, shoving it around with his spoon.

Becca gazed at Brandon with unabashed

adoration. I made a mental note to talk to her about not being so transparently in love. The February *Teen Time* magazine my mom brought home from work cautioned against it. She worked at McQuen's drugstore, and if magazines didn't sell, she brought them home for me. Sure, the covers were torn off, and they were a month old, but they were free and full of sage advice.

"Fluffnstuff is missing," Bran said with a frown. "Lana's cocker spaniel."

I sucked in my breath. Missing was not good. I leaned forward to catch any details about the disappearing dog.

I, Gabby St. Claire, am an amateur sleuth.

"Pete will fill you in on the details." Brandon stuffed a forkful of mashed potatoes in his mouth.

Pete plunked his tray on the other side of Becca and swept his blond hair that spilled over his blue eyes back from his face. He wore a much-washed Spiderman T and faded jeans. His face was clouded over like the sky before a thunderstorm.

"Did Fluff get out of the yard?" I asked.

"No." Pete shook his head, his mouth set in a firm line. "He was being boarded at the

Oceanside Vet Clinic. My family went to Richmond last weekend because Lana had another dance competition. Mom and Dad didn't want my cousin watching our place because they think he's become too irresponsible. So what happens? The irresponsible clinic lost him."

"Lana cried all last night," Brandon inserted, his eyes showing worry.

"She refused to go to school today so she could look for him," Pete added.

"Your parents let her skip school to look for her dog?" Becca put down her tuna sandwich in disbelief. Her parents would likely make her attend school right after triple bypass surgery. They were that strict.

"No. They made her go, but they might as well have not bothered. She'll cry the whole time, get sent to the office, and get sent home, if I know my sister. She's an actress to the core."

"What did the clinic people have to say?" I asked.

Pete shrugged and stabbed at his mac and cheese, jerking his head at Brandon. Becca leaned ever so slightly against Brandon's shoulder like she was having a hard time hearing. I bet even with icky cafeteria food surrounding us, she could smell his sandalwood-and-leather scent, my favorite mixture. Of course, had he been more of a musk-and-Ivory-soap guy, that would have been my favorite combination.

"Get this." Brandon dropped his voice like he was sharing a national secret. "Not just Fluff, but two other dogs disappeared from Oceanside also. There was no sign of a break-in, and no other pets were missing."

"This guy who had his pit bull boarded there said he was going to sue them," Pete said.

"That could put them out of business and start a downward spiral of the local, circular economy," Becca added.

Everyone turned to stare at my BFF. Sometimes the strangest things came out of her mouth. It was like she actually paid attention in classes and applied what she was learning to real life.

Which was probably why she was a straight-A student—if you didn't count her B in pre-algebra. And no one in their right mind would count it because everyone in the entire Hampton Roads region knew that not even Einstein could get an A from Ms. Lynnet. I was lucky to be carrying a C minus in her torture chamber.

Mental note: When you have that talk about not staring so obviously at Brandon, mention about how talking like a normal kid is a good idea, too.

"I don't care if they do go out of business. If they can't keep people's pets safe, they should be shut down." Pete was so agitated that a cheesy macaroni shot off his plate, bounced off my juice box, and landed in my lap.

"Sorry."

"No prob." I flicked the wayward noodle onto the floor.

Just then the fifth member of our BFFL group gently set her tray to my left. Paulette Zollin's somewhat vacant look was the only thing that detracted from her picture-perfect platinum blonde hair, expensive clothes, and classically beautiful face. Today her pale tresses were swept up and away from her face with two silver combs sparkling with red stones. Unlike most middle-school bling, Paulette's were the real thing because her parents were so rich they probably lent Bill Gates money.

Normally, hot guys and rich girls do not gravitate to fringers like Becca and me. Becca was brainy enough for the Geeks or Readers, but not me. We weren't Jocks, Skaters, Punks, or Emos. I might have hung with the Trolls since I frequently got detention for unavoidable tardies and occasionally for saying the first thing I thought of in class. But I didn't get in serious trouble, so I didn't fit with the Mocha Locos, Goths, or Heads.

It was a good thing being in a recent production of *Oklahoma* had brought us together and, much to my surprise and delight, seemed to be keeping us together, because otherwise Becca and I would still be fringers.

"Pete and I are going to put up some reward signs after school. You guys want to help?" Brandon asked.

"Absolutely," I blurted out, jumping at an excuse to hang with Bran.

Then I mentally checked my calendar. Not that I had many pressing social engagements, but detention did factor into my plans more often than I'd like. Thankfully, I'd been on time recently.

Becca squirmed in her seat. Her face made it evident that she would willingly look for the competition's dog if it meant spending time with Bran the Man, but something was holding her back. Probably her parents. Her dad was an ex-marine who just joined the Virginia Beach police force. To say they kept a tight rein on Becca would be like saying the ocean was a little wet. They had pulled her out of our production of *Oklahoma* over that one measly B in pre-algebra.

"Um, I'll have to meet you guys somewhere," she mumbled. "That is, if I can."

"I have Equestrian Club." Paulette sounded sincerely sorry.

I couldn't help thinking how awesome it would be to go horseback riding so often you were part of a club. Plus, if the stuff on TV was accurate, they got to wear these cute, form-fitting outfits complete with black riding helmets.

"No prob," Pete said. "Where should we meet up?"

Pete's blue eyes met mine, and I felt a little tingle run up my spine and grab my tongue. Which is the only reason I stuttered when I said, "Uhhhh?"

Could that and my quickening pulse and flushing face have anything to do with Pete's gaze? Or his smile? I noticed for the first time he had really white, really straight teeth, high cheekbones, and a rounded chin. Compared to Brandon's lithe dancer build, he was more solid.

Did he like me? Did I like him?

No way. Brandon was my crush. Even if it

was my most carefully guarded secret.

"We could cover more ground on bikes," Brandon answered.

"Not with my bike," Pete said. "It's falling apart, but Dad has no time to help me fix it because he and everyone else are so busy shuttling Lana from play practice to voice class to dance." Pete frowned.

I knew what it was like to have a parent put all their time and effort into one of your siblings. It wasn't fun. But my situation was totally different than Pete's.

"When I get my license, I'll be glad to take over those duties." Brandon smiled and arched an eyebrow.

A frown momentarily crossed Becca's face at the mention of Lana's name, but she quickly recovered her composure. She'd be a great actress on the Oceanside Middle School stage one day, if her parents ever allowed her to have any fun.

"You ought to meet at the vet's. Start investigating at the scene of the crime," she suggested.

"I don't have a bike," I said, "so I'll meet you guys there."

My parents wouldn't know if I didn't make it

home right after school. Mom was working at McQuen's Drugs until ten, and Dad would be either napping, drinking, or zoned out in front of the TV.

"I will too, if I can," Becca said without much real conviction.

"We will find Fluff and save the day." Brandon's confidence was infectious.

Pete sat up straighter and squared his shoulders. "We'll end up heroes."

Pete and Brandon thumped fists before breaking into smiles. I found myself staring at Pete's lips just a little longer than necessary. The rest of lunch, we planned out our strategy and complained about homework.

"Let's do this, guys," said Pete as we stood to toss our trash.

It had been a comment to everyone, but he was looking at me. His eyes lingered a fraction of a second longer than necessary on mine. Heat surged through my face, my whole body. I hoped I wasn't coming down with the flu or anything.

Because I absolutely, positively could not be attracted to Pete.

CHAPTER 3

Brandon, Pete, and I stood inside the nearly empty lobby of the Oceanside Veterinary Clinic and Boarding. Even though only one customer holding a cat carrier was at the counter and another sat on a bench with a black Scottie dog on a red leash, the counter staff were hustling at a hectic pace, but waiting on no one. They seemed nervous, because they kept glancing around like storm troopers were about to invade.

The place smelled more of pine cleaner than the wet dog I expected after today's shower. I heard the barking of a single dog, probably small from the tinny sound it made, coming from the back.

Pete leaned toward me. "It's usually really busy in here," he whispered.

His breath smelled fruity from the gum he'd been chewing.

Oceanside Ghost Town.

A teenager in a white lab coat came through a door from the back and took the Scottie from his owner. The little dog's nails clicked across the tiled floor. The other customer glanced around the waiting room, shook her head, and left.

Brandon leaned in. "Looks like word got around about the missing mutts."

I nodded just as one of the counter staff hung up the phone and motioned us over.

"How can I help you?" she asked in a worn-out tone. Her shoulder drooped like my mom's did when she did a double shift or cleaned someone's house for extra cash.

Pete held up one of the reward signs that contained a picture of Fluffnstuff and contact information. "We want to hang this here, just in case someone has seen my sister's dog."

"And we have a few questions," I added, tapping into my inner detective.

"Who are you?" She frowned at me as she took the poster from Pete and pinned it on a corkboard with other flyers advertising grooming services and lost pets.

"I'm part of the search and rescue squad. I was wondering if we could take a look at where the dogs were kept." She was already starting to say "no," so I quickly added, "Just for a second. It's not like we'll be in the way."

"We're too busy to have kids underfoot." She turned and disappeared behind a door labeled Employees Only.

We stared at each other in disbelief.

"They're hiding something," I muttered as we headed out.

As the boys unlocked their bikes, I checked out the fenced area behind the clinic. White Coat was giving the Scottie a potty break. This was my chance, I decided. I sauntered over.

"Fun job?" I called over the fence.

White Coat shrugged and came toward me. Getting a closer look, I figured she might be in high school.

"Not really. I want to be a vet someday. I thought I'd get some hands-on experience working here. But the only things they let me do, my seven-year-old sister could do." She rolled her eyes in disgust.

Pete and Brandon pushed their bikes over to join me.

"Were you here over the weekend?" I asked, trying to sound casual.

Immediately her eyes darkened, and she glanced nervously back toward the building.

"No. Why are you asking?" She crossed her arms over her chest.

I decided I needed to tread carefully. I motioned to Pete. "His sister's dog is one of the missing ones. We tried to talk to the lady inside, but she blew us off. I guess she thinks we're just dumb kids."

White Coat relaxed, and I knew I'd struck a chord.

"We just wanted some info so we could search more effectively." I stared pointedly at Pete.

Our eyes locked. Electricity buzzed up my spine.

"My sister's pretty torn up about it. I just want to find Fluff but don't know where to start looking," Pete said.

Without words, he'd understood my silent message.

We might have a psychic connection.

"I'm really sorry." White Coat's voice softened and she uncrossed her arms, setting them on the fence. She jerked her head toward the building. "You have to have gray hair and sing along with elevator music to get respect around here. When I mentioned I thought it was strange the thieves completely ignored the drugs and the merchandise, they blew me off."

"So only three dogs were missing?" I asked. "Were they the only pets being boarded?"

"Just the three, and we were at capacity." She lowered her voice, even though we were the only ones within half a mile. "I think someone wanted those three dogs because they were male pedigreed show dogs."

"Won't the thieves get caught the minute they try to show them?" I asked.

"Yes. But if they are smart, they'll just breed them. People make a bundle on stud fees." She leaned closer. "The office manager is blaming Jenny, the weekend tech, saying she must have forgotten to lock up. But I know Jenny. She may be in high school too, but she's not an airhead. But since the police said there was no sign of a break-in, the others are convinced it's her fault."

"What kind of dogs were the others?" I asked.

"An Irish setter and a pit bull, both championship show dogs. The pit bull's owner is threatening a lawsuit for lost stud fees. He claims he makes as much as $5,000 a year breeding him." She glanced back at the building. "I gotta go. Good luck. I hope you find your dog."

Five thousand dollars sounded like a motive for dognapping to me.

CHAPTER 4

Twenty-four posters later, I jogged home to keep warm, but my mind raced at the speed of light. I kept wondering what it meant that Pete and I could have a wordless exchange while at the vet, especially since we'd known each other for less than a month.

I rounded the corner and caught sight of home, the left side of a white two story with a piece of cardboard taped to the lower right corner of the bay window. I wondered when my father was ever going to get around to fixing it. It made our duplex look so ghetto. I skipped the three cement stairs to the front door, glad to be getting out of the wind.

As soon as I stepped inside the house, my mom rounded the corner from the kitchen. Lines of worry were etched around her eyes. "Gabby! Where have you been? Your father and I called the school. They said you didn't stay back for an activity."

I'd forgotten this was her day off from work. *Ooops!*

"I was helping a friend look for their dog. We were putting up signs and stuff," I explained, hanging up my jacket. I tried to sound noble and needed so I wouldn't be in a whole lot of trouble. When Mom was off we ate right at 5:00 p.m. The kitchen clock stared at me, the 6:33 an accusation: *Bad Daughter.*

"I wish you had let us know. I was getting concerned," she called over the sound of the oven timer.

I caught the scent of garlic bread and a whiff of the wonderful aroma of her spicy lasagna wafting from the kitchen. Mom usually made something special on her nights off. It was part her wanting us to have dinner together as a family and part cooking lesson for yours truly. Between my inability to master much besides microwaving frozen food and Dad's eat-and-run-back-to-the-TV, I bet Mom felt like these suppers were a dining disaster.

And now I had added to that grief by being late. I vowed to pay better attention in the future and be especially complimentary tonight.

"My favorite. Thanks, Mom." I sneaked a peek under the aluminum-foil-covered pan. My mouth watered of its own accord, and I spontaneously gave her a big hug, hoping it would make up for my thoughtlessness.

"Wash up and call your dad." She raised both eyebrows and smiled like she knew a Christmas-sized secret. "I have some news that I think you'll like."

As I hurried to comply, my stomach urging me to waste no time, I wondered what her news might be. If it had been something positive in the missing persons case about my brother Timmy, she wouldn't have waited until we gathered around the table. It had been four years since he vanished from the neighborhood playground where I was supposed to be watching him.

I quickly jerked my mind away from going down that dark, awful alley. Instead I shook my dad, who was dozing in front of the TV, and took the stairs two at a time to wash up.

After my mom prayed and we'd heaped our plates with the still-steaming lasagna, I slathered margarine onto the garlic bread. A random thought popped into my head. Garlic bread gives you bad breath. *Teen Time* had cautioned against ever eating it if you were on a date.

What would it be like to go on a real date? I pondered that as I bit into a forkful of delicious, gooey cheese, pasta, and sauce. I imagined sitting at a little Italian café with red-and-white checkered tablecloths and a lit candle stuffed in an empty wine bottle. Sitting across from me was . . . Pete!

How did Pete get there? Ever since the play, it had been Brandon sitting there, holding my hand and gazing into my eyes.

I mulled over the afternoon's events. Pete had talked mostly to me, ranting about how Lana had hardly any time for her pet anymore since she was taking voice and dance lessons as well as being involved in choir and the drama club at Oceanside High. At first I thought it was kind of strange since he pretty much ignored Brandon to talk to me, but then I figured it was because Brandon wouldn't want to hear complaining about his girlfriend.

But what if it was because he wanted to talk to *me,* not Brandon? Could Pete like me? And what about that mind-reading thing? Did that mean we were destined for each other?

"Gabby, have you heard a word I said?" My mom sounded frustrated.

I scrambled for a reply that would keep me out of trouble.

"Can't think of anything but how good this

tastes, Mom."

My mom smiled, but I knew she knew I'd said it as a save.

"A charmer, just like your dad," she answered. "The Wrangleys understandably didn't want to leave Pocococo at Oceanside Boarding. So, what do you say?"

I still was clueless. Pocococo must be the Wrangleys' pet, but I still didn't know what my mom was asking me. With a flash of brilliance that surely rivaled that of Sherlock Holmes and Albert Einstein on their best days, I replied, "So exactly how does this involve me? Like in detail."

"Help me clean up here, and I'll take you over to *show* you exactly what you'll have to do," my mom said, gathering dirty plates.

I swiped another piece of buttery garlic bread, took a bite, and pitched in.

"Great meal, Bobbi. I'm going to catch the news," Dad said, kissing my mom's cheek.

Then he left us to do all the work. My mom beamed at his compliment, and some of her weariness seemed to melt away.

My dad wasn't much help around the house, but he was still a charmer when he wanted to be.

I pushed that thought aside. Now, what

could this news be that my mom was so excited about?

CHAPTER 5

It was two minutes after 8:00 p.m., the Chapmans' deadline for Becca to get phone calls. But since my BFF had called me twice while Mom and I were at the Wrangleys' and since technically I'd be returning her calls, I decided to risk it. Plus, I was desperate to share all my news and talk about Pete.

I dialed as I dashed up the stairs and into my bedroom chatting corner. I kicked aside some laundry and lay on the floor, plopping my sock feet on my bed, and cushioning my head with an overstuffed pillow.

A gruff male voice answered, and my heart sank. But I gave it my best shot.

"Hi, Mr. Chapman. It's Gabby. I'm returning Becca's call. Tell her my math book and skills are at her disposal." I hoped my cheery greeting and math reference might make him more kindly disposed to let us talk.

"I'll get her," he said.

I breathed a sigh of relief.

"But try to keep it short," he continued. "It's a school night, so she has to be off by 8:30."

"Yes, sir." I would have saluted through the phone if I could.

Classical music from the local public broadcasting station played in the background. I wasn't sure which would be worse: the absence of a television or the constant presence of weird, dead-people music.

Evening was my time to discuss the things you shared only with your BFF. I loved this time of night with the moonlight floating in through the window, painting my drab-by-daylight room with a silvery, otherworldly glow, tension melting out of my muscles and into the floor.

"Gabby! Where have you been? How did it go? You are so lucky! Did Brandon mention me? Like, 'Too bad Becca couldn't come' or anything? Tell me everything." Becca was trying to keep her voice low, but in her excitement she was squeaking.

I gave her a blow by blow about the visit to Oceanside Boarding and posting the flyers. I was dying to dish about my crime-busting theories, my new job, and especially the Pete possibility, but Becca kept backtracking for details like

"What was Brandon's expression when he said that?" or "Are you sure he and Lana aren't having any, even the tiniest, problems?"

Finally, only when her dad bellowed, "Five more minutes," was I allowed to get a word in edgewise. But then it was too late. Even though I was dying to talk about Pete, caution locked my tongue. I didn't want to look foolish if I was imagining the whole Pete thing.

Instead, I brought up my theories about the disappearing dogs. "So, I'm wondering if someone stole the dogs to breed them, you know, to avoid all those stud fees. What do you think?"

"Seems pretty risky. It could be a disgruntled employee."

I frowned. "A grunting employee? What do you mean?"

"Not grunting, disgruntled. You know, unhappy. Dad says he's more concerned this is someone trying to make a statement and this may just be the beginning."

"Like who, and a statement about what?" I asked.

"Like a competitor, another boarding company that wants to take their business. Didn't Mr. C. tell your class about the economic principles of competition in the marketplace?"

I could have explained that half of what our teacher said went over my head and the other half I just ignored, but we were short on time. I didn't want to waste any on a lecture about being a better student. Plus, it seemed like a good segue into what was going on in my life.

"Yeah, I think so, but speaking of competition, I am the competition. I am a professional pet sitter. Like, I'm getting paid seven dollars every morning and every evening for walking and feeding the Wrangleys' pets and doing some other random, easy stuff like taking the trash to the curb and bringing in the mail."

"Wow! You lucked out twice today. I am so jealous! What kind of dog?"

"Pocococo is this adorable, skinny tan thing with huge black eyes. He loves to crawl up your arms to lick your face."

"That's great, Gabby. At fourteen dollars a day, you're hauling in twice what any babysitter our age makes in two hours."

The admiration and twinge of envy in her voice was gratifying, although I was a bit covetous of her math-whiz skills that figured out my income on the fly.

"Even if you put half the money in your

college fund, after the five days you'll have way more than you need to buy those silver spangled flip-flops you were admiring," Becca joked.

Last summer, I had gone with the Chapmans to the oceanfront for a day of sun, sand, and swimming. Becca and I had strolled the boardwalk, stopping to window-shop at a tourist trap with the most outrageous pairs of flip-flops I'd ever seen. The straps were covered with sequins, and a gaudy golden sunflower sprouted between your big toe and the next. The twenty-five-dollar price tag had sent us into hysterics.

I considered myself a connoisseur of flip-flops since I owned seven pairs, one for each day of the week. But my most expensive pair, the ones that left a barefoot imprint behind, ran me four dollars, tops. Not even I would plunk down that kind of serious money unless the gold was twenty-four karat.

"I was planning to wait until the flip-flops went on sale. They'd have to drop them to at least $24.98 before I'd consider buying them," I said in mock seriousness.

We both giggled.

Then I added as casually as I could, "Pete said maybe he and I could put some more flyers around tomorrow when Brandon is at dance class. What do you think of that?"

"I think I'd like to be at that dance class," Becca joked. Then she added more seriously, "Didn't you say you guys hung about thirty flyers already?"

"Yeah. It seems like overkill to me too." I hesitated, but my curiosity won over caution. I had to get her opinion. "Pete asked for my phone number and gave me his. He said it was in case someone called about the dog, but . . ."

"But what?"

My mouth was suddenly as dry as the Sahara Desert, but I forged on. "Do you think maybe hanging more flyers is an excuse to hang out with me? Or maybe he got my number for another reason?"

I held my breath. Sometime in the last six hours, my heart began wanting Pete to like me as more than a friend. In fact, I hadn't gone into a Brance once in the last two hours. I hoped I wasn't reading more into it than I should and wouldn't end up looking like a fool.

"I don't know. Let me think about it," Becca said pensively. "Better yet, I'll watch him tomorrow at lunch, you know, when he doesn't know I'm watching."

I let out the breath I didn't know I was holding.

"Really?" I asked with my best mock disbelief. "Be for real, girlfriend. Since when can you tear your eyes away from Bran the Man for even a second? Remember last week when you nearly poked your eye out with your straw because your peepers were glued to his face?"

We both giggled again.

"Sounds like you've moved on from math. Time to wrap it up." Mr. Chapman's ex-marine voice came through loud and clear even if he was in another room and who knew how much telephone wire away.

"Later, gator," Becca said, her voice flattening with disappointment.

But she wasn't nearly as disappointed as I was. I could have easily spent another hour chatting about the Pete possibility.

Instead I answered, "Down the road, toad."

"In a blizzard, lizard," she whispered and hung up.

I lay staring out of the window at the darkened sky for a while and mulled things over.

Did I like Pete or did I just want a boyfriend, any boyfriend? What would it be like to have a boyfriend? Would I know what to say? What to do?

I dug around my closet until I found the diary Becca had given me for Christmas. Truth be told, I hadn't used it to record my most secret thoughts but instead as my own private theater dictionary and a crime investigation notebook when I solved my first mystery a couple of months ago. If I wasn't going to get a word in edgewise with Becca, maybe the diary would have to do.

As I donned my flannel PJs, I decided instead I'd better spend some extra time brushing and flossing so I didn't have garlic breath.

How long does garlic stay on your breath? Would it still be there tomorrow at lunch?

How do you manage to eat garlic bread and have a boyfriend?

CHAPTER 6

On Thursday, a tall, skinny white man wearing a lab coat nervously fiddled with the dark-rimmed glasses perched on his long, thin nose. He was quite the contrast with Ms. Shernick, our even-keeled African American science teacher. Using my fabulous powers of deduction, I surmised he was our speaker for Career Day.

As I took my seat, I noticed one of my lab partners, Hannah, was scowling at him. I did a double take since Hannah rarely reacted to anything, not even when she first came to OMS and the Diva asked her if her clothes were Amish or *Little House on the Prairie* castoffs.

Ms. Shernick rapped a plastic graduated cylinder on her desk to get our attention. "Class, this is Dr. Arnold from Pollack Laboratories. He is filling in for the original speaker, who is out with the flu."

Without raising his hand, Raff Valentini Diaz

called out, "So, we're supposed to think you drug guys know wassup, but your guy is home sick? Guess your drugs don't work so good."

Most of the class began to giggle at his impertinent joke but immediately halted when Ms. Shernick's mouth flattened into a hard line. She drilled Raff with her eyes like a Texan drills for oil.

"That will be enough," she said sharply.

Raff coolly leaned back in his seat, raising his hands in mock surrender.

"Umm, well. Good day, students." Dr. Arnold rocked back and forth on the balls of his feet and rubbed his hands. "I'm not a biologist like many of the scientists at the lab, nor am I a chemist. I'm a geologist. Does anyone know what a geologist specializes in?"

A few hands shot up, but Dr. Arnold ignored them.

"Geology. Minerals. We study earth science and rocks, of course, but I specialize in minerals." His voice quivered, and he gave a nervous smile.

I felt a little bad for him. He probably felt far more comfortable with a bunch of stones than the rock-brained students staring at him or doodling.

"This is Mohs' hardness scale," he said, pointing to a chart. "We rate rocks on how scratch resistant they are. Talcum powder, which is used to make baby powder, is a one. Gypsum, from which we get plaster of Paris for casts, is a two. Has anyone here ever had a cast?"

A couple students raised their hands.

I zoned out, trying to figure out what had gone wrong at lunch. True to her word, Becca tried to observe the interaction between Pete and me this week, but there was very little. Today Pete seemed even more aloof and distracted, pushing his peas around his meatloaf and grumbling about Lana.

My concentration was broken as someone plopped a baggie onto my desk. It looked like flour, but the label identified it as talc. I passed it to Hannah, who took it without looking. Her scowl had turned into a hard stare like Dr. Arnold was the devil in disguise.

"Drug companies rarely have interest in rocks harder than four. Can anyone guess why?" Dr. Arnold looked around hopefully, but no one was really paying attention. "Let me give you a clue. It has to do with solutes and solvents."

A clue. That's what we needed about the disappearing dogs. Though my interest had started because I wanted to spend more time with Brandon, now a new curiosity burned inside me. I wanted answers, on more than one level.

Was it an inside job by an unhappy employee at Oceanside Vet? A competitor from another local boarding facility? Someone making a statement? A broke dog breeder? If the dogs were stolen by someone wanting to dognap specific dogs, the perp (as Becca's dad called criminals) would have had to know those three dogs would be there and that they had value as breeding stock.

Plop. Another baggie, this time containing a finer white dust, dropped on my desk. Gypsum.

"Do any of you or your parents have indigestion and use tablets you can drop into a glass of water?" Poor Dr. Arnold was trying to make his presentation relevant and interesting, but no one really cared.

The Diva, always the attention-grabbing social butterfly of the entire seventh grade, must have seen this as an opportunity to score some attention and brownie points, because she raised her hand.

"Yes, Donabell?" Ms. Shernick waved a hand in her direction.

The Diva sat ramrod straight, pausing to make sure she had everyone's undivided attention. She cleared her throat and meaningfully glanced at the new girl. The new girl—the one who had protected her orange, bobbed hair from the downpour last Monday—immediately froze in her seat and dropped her eyes like a submissive mutt.

It's pathetic what some people will do to fit in.

"My father is a doctor, so I'm quite aware of medications," Donabell started.

Dr. Arnold scrunched his eyebrows together in what appeared to be confusion. "Very good. Most antacids are made of calcite, number three on Mohs' hardness scale," he continued. "This means the manufacturer can use effervescent tablets that dissolve in water."

Next to me Hannah muttered, "They use things, all right. They use animals to test their products."

Her hands were clenched in her lap, and one foot was popping up and down, up and down like a piston. I had never seen her so worked up.

Dr. Arnold didn't seem to hear her. "Fluoride, at four, can be dissolved in toothpastes to help strengthen teeth. That could never happen with hard minerals like rubies, sapphires, and diamonds."

"Diamonds . . . now you're talking my kind of language. Small, easy to slip in a pocket, and good resale value, if you get my drift," Raff commented.

He stretched and eased the leg encircled with a gleaming ankle monitor into the aisle. Raff, two years older than the rest of us, loved to show it off like it was Olympic gold.

Dr. Arnold, grinning broadly, not only missed the monitoring device, he missed the fact Raff was trying to disrupt, not add to, class. "Yes, diamonds are very hard. They are a ten, the top of Mohs' scale. Rubies and sapphires are a nine. They all come from metamorphic rocks, and any of them will scratch glass. But pharmaceutical companies don't use them."

Hannah erupted out of her seat like lava spewing from a volcano. "Drug companies use poor, helpless animals kept caged up in horrible conditions. You test things on them. How can you sleep at night knowing your so-called research brings pain, suffering, and death to so many of God's creatures?"

She crossed her arms and waited for him to reply.

Dr. Arnold's mouth started moving up and

down, but no sound came out.

"That is enough." Ms. Shernick's sharp tone woke up all the sleepers. "Take your seat, Hannah."

"You wouldn't like it if you had no choice and had to be a test dummy." Hannah's voice rose in intensity and volume. "People take their cats, dogs, or puppies to shelters thinking they'll be adopted to a loving family, but instead they go to your labs."

The whole class stared at her like she had three eyes or alien antennae sprouting from her head. Raff was muttering something about a *loco mamacita*.

"Oh no," Dr. Arnold interjected. "We raise our own mice, rats, and rabbits. We don't use people's pets. In fact, I'm an avid supporter of Paws and Furballs, the local animal rights organization. I serve on their board of directors, as a matter of fact."

Hannah grabbed a bunch of papers of her desk and shook them above her head. "Liar! These are confirmed reports and news articles from reliable sources. Pollack Laboratories was busted several times for not only using shelter animals but stealing pets from people's yards." Her eyes roamed over the entire class. "These people are monsters. Monsters in our midst."

"Hannah. Outside. Now!" Ms. Shernick's firm voice took control.

Hannah slammed the papers onto her desk and strode out, eyes locked onto poor Dr. Arnold the whole time. The force she used caused some of the papers to slide off her desk and onto the floor around my feet. I gathered them up and took a peek since my curiosity was aroused.

Could these papers hold a clue about the disappearing dogs? Was Pollack Labs somehow involved?

One was a photocopy of a *Los Angeles Times* article dated July 15, 1946, with the picture of a mushroom cloud. The headline read "Atomic Animals." I scanned the print. The government's testing of nuclear weapons in the Nevada desert included dogs and human soldiers. Another paper from the Humane Society of America denounced the use of animals in laboratories, especially if procured from animal shelters.

I ignored Ms. Shernick's attempt to get the class refocused and Dr. Arnold soothed enough to carry on with his presentation. I placed the papers on Hannah's desk and nonchalantly snuck another one off her desk and onto mine. It was a photocopy of an email from Pollack Labs requesting donations of "live nonhuman test subjects." I scanned it for a date but couldn't find one.

The thought seemed like a whim just a few minutes ago. But what if there was a connection? What if Pollack Labs was behind the missing dogs?

CHAPTER 7

"I'll be thrilled when you have a driver's license and can chauffeur Lana to this, that, and another thing," Pete mumbled to Brandon as they parked their lunch trays on Friday. "You have no idea what it's like to babysit my little sister Suzy while Mom's running Lana all over."

"But I do," said Brandon, obviously wanting to tease him. "I heard you love playing My Little Ponies so much you're gonna get a rainbow tattoo."

Becca giggled appreciatively while I tried my best to keep a straight face.

"Puddles chewed up most of my old My Little Ponies, but I can let you have the other ones," Paulette offered in all sincerity. "I don't play with them anymore."

My self-control dissolved, and I joined in the laughter that erupted. Pete's eyebrows knit together as he scowled at us, but poor Paulette glanced around like she was lost in the Bermuda

Triangle and trying to use a map written in Swahili to get out.

"I have a better idea. Why don't I give Puddles an entire herd of those stupid things to chew. Puddles is a puppy, right?" Pete offered.

He'd hardly said two words all week, and Becca and I had concluded the romance between us was a figment of my imagination.

"No. She is a Yorkie."

"Is she a show dog?" Becca asked, opening her sack lunch.

"No. It would make her too nervous. Almost everything makes her scared, and then she has an accident. That's how she got her name. But it's not her fault. It was because the puppy millers made her have too many batches of puppies."

"Paulette, you adopted a dog with bladder problems?" I asked. This made no sense to me at all. "You could afford the perfect dog. Why one that pees all over?"

"My parents didn't want me to adopt her. They said to pick another one. But I felt bad that she had been in that horrible puppy mill place. When I saw Puddles, she just looked at me like she was saying, 'Give me a chance. I might be slow, but I'll learn.' So I insisted, and Daddy gave in."

"You got her from a puppy mill?" Becca asked. "Those places are horrible. When people buy animals from them, it just keeps them in business."

"They are awful, and that's why Paws and Furballs busted them, but then they had all these dogs and puppies and not enough room to keep them," Paulette explained. "Daddy's on their board of directors, and he took me with him to see about it."

"What exactly is Paws and Furballs?" I asked. Goofy Dr. Arnold had mentioned the organization, and it seemed like I'd heard their name somewhere before. Maybe they were connected to the disappearing dogs.

"It is a local agency that stops animal cruelty," Becca said, then turned mischievously to Pete and added, "I might have to report you for cruelty to My Little Ponies."

Everyone laughed again. The bell ending lunch rang, so we scurried to clean up and move out.

"Gabby?"

I looked over, wondering if I'd really heard my name in all the noise. I had. It was Pete. My heart started to thud like I'd run a three-minute mile.

"I wanted to say sorry if I blew you off at lunch this week," Pete said. "Bran said I was pretty rude to everyone."

"No prob," I said casually and unsure of what to say next. Usually my problem was stopping myself from saying too much, but around Pete, I was at a loss for words.

"You're pretty lucky, you know, being the only child. You get all the attention you want. When you're the middle kid, you're easy to overlook," Pete blurted out. He sounded mad and hurt at the same time.

I didn't say what I was thinking—that I wasn't an only child, that I had a brother and he had disappeared without a trace, just like Lana's dog. It was a dark and gloomy thought, and I shivered involuntarily. Pete must have noticed.

"Sorry I unloaded like that," he apologized. "I'm being rude again. Listen, I also wanted to ask if you wanted to go with me Saturday to post a few more flyers. We could meet here at school."

"Yeah, okay," I managed, my heart doing cartwheels.

Wow! It was kind of like a date, wasn't it? He could have asked everyone at the table, but he'd waited until it was just the two of us. That had to mean something.

"Great. See you tomorrow, then." Pete nodded and angled off towards his class.

He was half a hallway away before I thought of something to say.

"You can unload to me anytime," I called after him.

He gave me a thumbs-up but didn't turn back around. I was so busy staring I ran into the Diva.

"Watch it, dorkina," she snapped.

For once the words bounced off harmlessly.

I might be going on a date!

I raced home after school to call Becca and couldn't believe it when Mr. Chapman said she was on phone restriction for a whole week. I had to talk to someone about this new development, but my mom was at work. Dad was sleeping in front of some old, old black-and-white movie entitled *The Hound of the Baskervilles.*

In the flick, Sherlock Holmes investigated a murder and a curse connected to a kidnapped girl in the 1700s. Helping him was a guy named Dr. Watson. I couldn't get into it, so I trudged upstairs and moped around my room.

I was tossing clothes into "wash" and "don't

wash" piles when I stumbled across the diary. I once again felt guilty about not using it much, but I just couldn't get past the whole dumb "Dear Diary" thing. Who writes to "Dear Diary"? It sounded way too close to diarrhea. Gross.

Then it hit me!

I was a detective like Sherlock Holmes. I needed a Dr. Watson to bounce things off of.

I opened the diary and began to write.

Dear Watson . . .

CHAPTER 8

Normally I'd sleep in on a Saturday, but today I had two reasons to get up: One, I had a job to do. Two, I kind of, might sort of, have a date. That was the conclusion Watson and I had reached last evening.

Pete had called last night to change our meet up to Oceanside Vet. Watson and I couldn't decide if he really wanted to change or if he just wanted to call me.

It was my first call from a boy-possible-boyfriend. He didn't say much except the meeting-up stuff, but it was enough to keep me awake half the night. I felt irritable and groggy when the alarm blared at 7:00 a.m.

I rolled out of bed and threw on some random clothes. There'd be time to shower and change into something cute before I met Pete.

The cold slapped me awake as I stepped outside. I jogged to Wrangleys' in order to save time and stay warm. The Wrangleys lived in a two-story house in a snooty neighborhood. When they'd given me a tour of the house, I'd noticed the upstairs only had one bedroom. The other two rooms were used as an office and home gym, complete with weights and a treadmill. I imagined they were an older couple and pretty well off because they had nice furniture and TVs in almost every room. Not that I was snooping. I was simply sharpening my powers of observation and deduction.

Pocococo danced around on his spindly hind legs when he saw me. We took a quick walk, because neither of us were fans of the cold, then headed inside so I could feed him and Wendell, the invisible cat who never poked a whisker out when I was there.

The only evidence of Wendell was the "presents" he left in the litter box. Still, I congratulated myself on my powers of observation and deducing the cat was still alive and well.

"Pocococo, I gotta go, but I'll be back tonight and tell you all about how things went with Pete." Having to discuss my love life with a dog and a diary named Dr. Watson just wasn't going to cut it long term, so I hoped Becca would get off restriction ASAP.

As I hustled home, I tried to figure out what I could wear that would a) look cute, b) make me look cute, and c) not be an obvious attempt to look cute.

An hour and fifty outfits later I settled on an emerald-green pullover sweater and my newest jeans. I pulled on my dress boots—warm brown suede ones with no heel. For good measure, I dabbed some perfume from one of the almost empty drugstore-brand testers my mom had brought home for me. The scent of Fragrant Fields, a mixture of Granny Smith apples, jasmine, and bamboo, wasn't in-your-nose obvious, but I hoped it would prove subtly alluring.

Pete beat me to the vet's. When I pulled up, he was kneeling beside his bike, and I couldn't tell if he was trying to adjust the chain or put it back on. I tried to think of some catchy greeting, but when nothing came to mind I settled for "hey."

Pete straightened, smiled, and jerked a thumb toward the gate to the run behind the clinic. "New padlock. Not much security, if you ask me, but I guess it is something."

The chain-link fence was only waist high.

The lock wouldn't stop someone from getting in or out, but it might slow them down if they were carrying a cocker spaniel like Fluff.

Pete must have been thinking the same thing, because after quick glances right and left, he vaulted over and back.

Our minds are really in tune!

"I'd like to get a closer look at the back door. Becca's dad mentioned something about thieves getting in with a credit card, but I don't see how that would work," I admitted.

Pete just chuckled.

"That's because you don't have snoopy siblings. Suzy has a bunch of those fake card things our parents get in the mail. She carries them around in her My Little Pony purse. She figured out how to slide one between the door and side of the doorway to get into Lana's room. Lana blew a gasket when she found Suzy sampling all her makeup."

"So the thief could have gotten through the back door that way?"

"Maybe so," Pete began.

The back door to Oceanside Vet opened, and Counter Woman from Monday let six dogs out. She spotted us and charged over.

"Just what are you doing here?" The

accusation in her voice left no doubt she thought we were up to no good. With her hands on her hips, she glared back and forth between us.

Pete pulled a reward poster from his back pocket and held it up. "Just came by to see if you guys had any more information on my sister's dog. That you guys lost."

"No, we don't know anything new." She frowned and turned away, dismissing us to clean up after the pooping pups.

I was glad I only had one dog to poop scoop for. I would hate cleaning up after the forty or so Oceanside could have if they were full. It sounded like an awful job.

"Let's go before she accuses us of being dognappers," Pete whispered.

I nodded and followed him, my heart skipping a beat at the thought of spending more time with Pete.

Suddenly, I had more than one reason to get involved: I wanted to find the missing dogs in case they were in danger. But I always looked forward to having an excuse to spend more time with Pete.

CHAPTER 9

Pete and I ended up near the Seaside Mall just after noon. It wasn't a real mall, just one of those touristy strip malls that seemed as dormant as the leafless trees in winter. Several of the places had Closed signs in the windows, and business crawled at the ones that were open. The guy at the Seaside Surf Shop recognized me from when my dad brought Tim and me to work there on Saturdays, and let us post our last flyer.

Pete kicked at his bike in disgust. "Either Dad is going to have to fix it or I need a new bike. This one is for the birds."

"I'm thinking about buying one with my pet-sitting money," I said. "It might be fun to ride some of the trails around here. Have you done any?"

I was hoping Pete would suggest cycling some together.

"Nah. Not with this piece of junk." Pete ran his hands through his wind-tousled blond hair, then stuffed them in the front of his Captain America hoodie. He cleared his throat and shuffled his feet. "What do you say we grab some lunch?"

My mouth went bone dry, as dry as a Bedouin's flip-flop. In the Sahara. During a drought. I felt a sudden overwhelming urge to sit down because my heart had stopped beating. I couldn't think of a response.

Gabby, get a grip. Answer him.

"Umm, uh, I didn't bring my purse," I stuttered, mentally kicking myself for sounding like a dorkina.

"No prob. I gotcha covered." Pete's voice came from a million miles away.

I barely managed a nod. My heart thumped like a rabbit's leg on steroids. I wanted to say something cool and eloquent and funny, but both my brain and my lips locked into shutdown mode.

Is this a date?

"It can be, if you want it to be," answered Pete.

Twenty bazillion thoughts flooded into my mind like Christmas shoppers storming a mall the day after Thanksgiving. Two clamored the loudest for immediate attention.

Did I just say that out loud?

I'm on a date!

But these were quickly swept aside as the others, some only fragments, shoved and elbowed for attention.

I am the world's biggest blabbermouth. How could I have let that slip?

Do I have windblown hair? Working deodorant? Will something get stuck in my teeth?

How can I talk if my mouth won't work? I don't know how to go on a date. Can I find a restroom, fix my hair, and call Becca? Dairy King.

Dairy King? Why am I thinking about Dairy King?

I wasn't. Pete had said the words aloud. I took a wild guess that was where he wanted to eat and nodded, following him on Jell-O legs.

CHAPTER 10

Twenty minutes later, my tongue still smarted from biting into my hot-off-the-grill hamburger too soon. I figured it was some sort of weird justice for betraying me when I blurted out, "Is this a date?"

What kind of mindless moron asks a guy if he's asking her on a date? Only a certified dorkina, that's who.

While I cooled my still-burning tongue with chocolate ice cream, I gave mental thanks that I had paid attention when Becca and I read in *Teen Time* that the best thing to do on a first date was to get the guy to talk about himself. I would never have guessed Pete could talk so much about Pete. I couldn't even remember the exact question that had unleashed his tongue, but I was beginning to feel like I was Pete's psychotherapist rather than his date.

"If it's not all about Lana, then it's Suzy, because she's the baby. I just wish for once they'd decide a weekend would be about—" Pete paused for a millisecond, not nearly long enough for me to add to the conversation. "No, I could live with just a day, for them to have a day that was all about Pete."

Pete's untouched sundae had melted into a gooey jumble of sprinkles, gummy bears, and Red Hots drowning in a vanilla sea. He drummed his spoon on the surface, submerging four gummy bears. I hoped it was just coincidence and not some unconscious desire to drown his family.

"One day I'm going to do something, something big, and they'll actually notice I exist."

Pete finally lifted a spoonful of his vanilla soup, so I cleared my throat and spoke, hoping I didn't have lettuce stuck between two teeth. "I think it is awful that parents say they love all their kids the same, but when it comes down to it, they all have favorites."

I didn't add that I had to compete for attention with a sibling who hadn't set foot in our house for four years. Pete might think I was nuts. I finished the last bite of my waffle cone.

"Yeah, you got that right. I mean, I'd get it if Lana or Suzy had cancer or something. Then I think it's okay for a kid to be center stage all the time, for whatever time they had left. It sucks being in the middle, 'cuz it's, like, never gonna be your time."

Not knowing what to do with my hands now that my cone was gone, I reached for the toothpick stabbed through my unwanted pickle. Pete reached out and took my hand in his.

He's holding my hand. The panic started up again, but at least I was sitting this time.

Did he think I was reaching for his hand? Is my palm sweaty? What do I do?

Noise burst through the glass doors as a ginormous herd of little kids poured off a YMCA of Richmond bus and into the fast food joint.

Pete squeezed my hand and let go, saying, "Time for us to blow."

I was both disappointed and relieved: disappointed because my first date was ending too soon, and relieved because it was ending before I'd done something incredibly stupid.

If this *was* absolutely, positively, a genuine, authentic first date.

CHAPTER 11

"You didn't!" Becca practically shouted on the other end of the phone.

"It just slipped out. I didn't mean to say it." I mentally kicked myself again for blurting out my dopey question. When would I ever learn to think before I spoke? "But he said it could be if I wanted it to. So what do you think? Was it a date or not?"

Please, please, let her think so. Please let it be real.

"I can't believe you said that," Becca persisted. "Although it's good to know the advice about getting the guy to talk worked out. He seemed pretty torqued at his parents, though."

"Becca!" I interrupted, my patience frayed and frazzled by the suspense. "Was it a date or not? Is Pete my boyfriend? Inquiring minds want to know."

"Okay, okay. Let's think this through logically. Pete isn't dating anyone else that we know of."

"Check."

"He paid."

"Check." I smiled, realizing things were looking up.

"Half a check," Becca corrected. "You told him you didn't have any money, so he might have paid since you were helping him out with the flyers, like when teachers buy chips and stuff for students who help clean their rooms at the end of the year."

"This is so not like a teacher bribing kids to help clean."

"He didn't ask you ahead of time or use the word *date*, but he held your hand. For how long?"

"Less than a minute," I admitted. "Why the YMCA had to pick Dairy King for lunch after the Virginia Aquarium has to be the worst possible coincidence ever."

"Yeah. Because if he'd held it for, say, three minutes or more, I think that would qualify."

I thought about asking if the three-minute time span was arbitrary or from a magazine, but Becca plunged on. "I'd give it an 85 percent probability."

Eighty-five percent? Where did she come up with

that number?

"Gabby, just consider something, okay?" Becca's voice sounded strange, like she was going to deliver some bad news like "You have cancer" or "You have detention until you're twenty-one."

I waited, scrunching my eyes shut like they could filter out bad news.

"I'm just asking," Becca said.

That worried me even more. Sentences that started out that way were never ones you wanted to hear.

"Had it ever crossed your mind that Pete had something to do with the missing dogs?"

It was not the bomb I'd been expecting; nevertheless I found myself sitting on the floor, my earring between my fingers instead of in my ear. I had no idea where the back had gone.

"Why in the world would you think that?" I asked.

"Sounds like Pete is desperate to get his parents' attention and make life hard for Lana in the process. That might qualify as motive. Plus, he brought up the credit-card-entry theory. Maybe because he used it."

"That's preposterous! Pete wouldn't do that. Besides, it was his sister who broke into Lana's room that way, not Pete."

"So he says. But be logical for a minute. His sister is seven or eight? Where would she learn that trick, except from, perhaps, an older brother?"

This conversation was not going anywhere I expected, not anywhere I wanted. I searched for something to say that would unequivocally prove Pete innocent of any wrongdoing. I came up empty.

"Gabby, you won't be the first girl that got taken in by a guy. My dad says serial killers fool people all the time. That's how they keep getting away with stuff."

"You think Pete is a serial killer?" I screeched. "Besides, your dad just got out of cadet school. He's no expert."

"He was military police in the Marine Corps for years," she snapped back.

Our heart-to-heart was turning mean. We never talked this way. I wanted a do-over on this conversation. I wanted to press "rewind" and start again, but I had to settle for "stop."

"Becca, I gotta go pet sit. Let's finish this later, gator."

"In an hour, sunflower."

"Maybe two, kangaroo." I hung up the phone

and headed to Wrangleys', hoping the walk and affectionate Pocococo would help me sort through and eliminate some of my new problems.

How could I have guessed it would make things a gazillion times worse?

CHAPTER 12

Thirty minutes later I found myself staring in horror at the crippled, homeless bum leaning on a cane on the Wrangleys' porch. Except for Pocococo, who was wiggling to get down, I was utterly alone. The street was as unoccupied as a ghost town, and I couldn't just run away, leaving my keys dangling from the front door.

The mysterious stranger might notice them and be able to figure out where I lived and break in, even with his bad leg. If he was a crazy, he might kill us all in our sleep.

On the other hand, if I didn't leave, I was never going to get to a phone and call for help.

"I'll call the cops if you try to dognap Pocococo. With that red hair you'll be easy to pick out of a lineup."

I had to figure out how he knew Pocococo's name! That could be an important clue for the police.

"Who are you and how did you get in? How

do you know this is Pocococo?" The fact that Poco had been sitting on the man's lap finally registered in my brain. It was possible he knew Poco and Poco knew him, but I wasn't taking any chances. This bum couldn't possibly be legit. The Wrangleys would have mentioned him. Or my mom. It wasn't like she could clean their entire house and *not* notice that scuzzball.

I swallowed. I was starting to perspire and, since the March weather was still lionlike, I knew it was fear that pulled it from my body. A gust of the wind tugged at my hair. Poco whined and tried to claw his way out of my grip.

What should I do? Why did I ever take this job?

"Look, *girl*." The bum's voice dripped with derision.

I bristled like an irate porcupine. The way he said *girl* was obnoxious, like I was a little kid or a weakling or both.

"I'm going inside out of this wind to call my sister," he continued. "Then I'm going to come back out and put the phone on the porch for you to talk to her. Then you're going to bring Pocococo back in the house." He stabbed his finger in the air, pointed right at me.

My mouth had gone dry, so instead of shouting something stupid, I had to summon up some moisture. In that split second, a brilliant plan coalesced in my mind.

While he's getting the phone, I'll get my keys and then make a run for it. I may not be a track star, but I can outrun a crippled bum.

I was a genius!

"Okay," I shout-squeaked.

The long-haired vagrant limped inside, closing the door behind him.

Yes!

I sprinted across the street, Pocococo tucked like a football in the crook of my arm. I hoped a car would round the corner or a neighbor would check their mail. Any sort of witness would be welcome right now.

No such luck. With the still-wiggling Pocococo squirming to get down, I glided up the steps and crossed the porch silently. I had almost extracted the keys when the door flew open and a steely hand latched onto my wrist like handcuffs.

I was off kilter, so trying to keep hold of Poco, regain my balance, and wrench myself out of the iron-fisted grip was impossible. Before I could even summon a scream, I found myself righted, Poco snatched out of my arm, and a cordless phone plopped into my now empty hand. The human handcuff let go.

I stepped backward, nearly falling down the three steps that led up to the house. A voice from far away was calling me.

The phone. The voice is coming from the phone.

"Gabby? Are you there, Gabby?"

It sounded like Mrs. Wrangley, but I wasn't sure. Cautiously, I put the phone to my ear and backed up a few more steps, still keeping my eye on the obnoxious man in front of me.

"Gabby?"

"Yes?" I finally said.

"Gabby, this is Mrs. Wrangley. Everything is fine, dear. Just relax."

Right. Relax, I thought sarcastically, racking my brain for a surefire way to determine if the caller really was Mrs. Wrangley or some henchman of the homeless burglar.

"Gabby, that's my brother, Amos, you just met. It's okay. I'm sorry if he gave you a start. We didn't expect him to drop by either."

The voice sounded like the lady I'd talked to a day and a half ago, but I wanted to make sure. "If you really are Mrs. Wrangley, who cleans your house and when?"

I backed down the steps, keeping my eyes on the vagrant stroking Poco's head.

"Your mother does, on Wednesday mornings."

"One more question: What kind of dog treats does Pocococo get?"

"None, because the vet has him on a diet." Mrs. Wrangley sounded amused.

My heartbeat started slowing down to normal. "Okay. I believe you."

Still, I stayed where I was, staring at the bum brother.

"Amos is going to be staying at our house for a few days. We had no idea he might drop in when we left for the funeral. Things here are getting complicated, so I'm not sure when we'll be home. But these things just seem to come in threes." Now Mrs. Wrangley sounded exasperated.

"And I am perfectly capable of taking care of the pets!" Amos shouted loudly enough for Mrs. Wrangley to hear.

"Gabby, dear, put Amos on the phone."

I held the phone out by the tip of the small plastic antenna and reluctantly eased it toward him. No way was I going to let him snag my wrist again, even if he was some black-sheep relative of the Wrangleys. He jerked the phone from me, scowling.

I got a good look at him then. He was wearing flip-flops, probably because the bulky bandage wrapped around his left foot, ankle, and calf wouldn't permit him to wear shoes. Between the top of the bandage and his knee, a tattoo peeked out. All I could tell was that it seemed to be a frog's head and the end of a trident, like the one I'd seen Neptune holding in mythology books.

"I can take care of a stupid dog and a cat, for heaven's sake. It's not like I'm in a wheelchair."

His legs were way too tan for March and way too muscled for me to have outrun him, had he not had the foot thing going on. I caught a whiff of Ivory soap and Bengay—not exactly what I'd expect from a guy that slept in a cardboard box in an alley. With all the facial hair it was hard to tell, but on closer inspection I guessed he was in his late twenties.

Poco, still trying to get down, was irritating the man. He shoved the dog into my hands and glared at me. "I don't need some *girl* showing up unannounced at all hours of the day and night, barging into the house."

He reached around inside the door and produced Poco's leash, which he held out. I took it, snapped the lead on, and let the dog down to take care of business in the front yard.

First, he scared me half out of my mind, and now he's getting me fired. It wasn't fair!

Amos held out the phone to me, so I took it, maintaining as much distance as possible between us.

"Gabby, I'm so sorry this happened," Mrs. Wrangley continued. "If we had had any idea, we would have let you know. I'm sure it was quite a shock to find a strange man in our house."

I wanted to fill her in on just how strange but wisely kept my mouth shut.

"If you would just take Poco for his walk one last time, Amos will manage the rest until we get home. I do so appreciate your willingness to jump in when we were in a tight spot. Do tell your mom about Amos, but I hope we'll be back before she cleans again. Unless we hit another speed bump. Thanks, Gabby."

"Uh, sure. Bye." The phone clicked off, and I glared at Amos. "Thanks for losing me my job."

Amos glowered back at me, then turned, hobbled inside, and shut the door. I quickly removed the keys and took Pocococo on his farewell walk.

CHAPTER 13

"It's just not fair, Mom," I wailed as I flopped into a kitchen chair. Canned TV laughter came from the living room, where I supposed my father was sleeping on the couch.

"Tootsie, there is no way any of us could have known. I know you are disappointed about the money, but look at the bright side. You'll be able to sleep in tomorrow." My mother was trying her best to be upbeat and cheerful as she mashed the potatoes.

My mom was like that. No matter how dismal the situation, Mrs. Bobbi St. Claire could find something to be happy about. I guess that came in handy with a husband like my dad and a kid like me. Sometimes I wished that just once, my mom would admit that life sucked. Before she could Pollyanna the situation further, the phone rang.

"I'll get it!" I yelled, hoping maybe it was Pete calling to ask me out on a real, bona fide, no-doubt-about-it date.

As I trotted off in the direction of the ringing, my mom called after me. "Don't stay on too long. This is the one night this week we can sit down and eat as a family . . . on time. And don't forget to put the phone back on the charger. You'll run the battery down otherwise."

I sighed as I searched for the phone. I usually was the one who forgot to put it where it belonged. Having to frequently hunt for a lost phone was about the only advantage to living in such a small space. It didn't help matters that one whole bedroom was off limits, being preserved as it was four years ago when my brother vanished.

Unhappy thought; don't go there.

I found the phone under my unfolded laundry on the ninth ring.

"Guess what, guess what, guess what?" To say Becca was excited was an understatement. "The police are having an auction of unclaimed bikes next week. Dad thinks you could get a pretty nice bike cheap. Then we could ride together."

"I can't," I snapped, mostly because of my disappointment that I'd lost my job and a teeny-weeny bit because it wasn't Pete.

"Of course you can. You're gonna be rolling in the dough."

"No, I'm not." I sighed.

"Why not?"

"Because I lost my job, therefore I am beyond broke."

"You got fired?" Becca's enthusiasm ebbed away. "What happened?"

One corner of my mouth turned up and my eyebrows knit together as I debated whether or not to point out that Becca, for once, had jumped to the conclusion I had been fired. I decided to let it go since I'd done enough jumping about Amos to make a trampoline dizzy.

"Turns out the Wrangleys' relative showed up, so they don't need me. Lucky me."

"Bummer. But they'll pay you for the dog walks you did do, won't they?"

"I guess. They better." I added more firmly, "Especially after what happened."

"Dinner, Gabby. Tell her you'll call back." Mom's voice floated upstairs.

"Okay, Mom." I reluctantly started back downstairs.

"Get off the phone. Don't keep your mother waiting," my dad growled, probably more hungry than concerned about my mom's feelings.

I rolled my eyes.

"Later, gator," I muttered.

"Soon, baboon."

I stomped a bit more than necessary on the rest of the stairs.

Mom said grace and tried to get a conversation going. Dad rarely had more to say than "pass the pepper," and I didn't have anything to say to him. I'd barely gotten the food on my plate when the phone rang again.

I jumped up to answer it, but my father pushed away from the table and barked, "I'll put an end to these interruptions."

He marched off toward the ringing.

I started to get up anyway, but my mom placed a gentle hand on mine. We both tensed when we heard him say, "We are having dinner," in a gruff tone.

I rolled my eyes and shoveled a forkful of hamburger and potatoes in my mouth. I was totally shocked when my father shuffled in and tossed the phone onto my lap. I gingerly picked it up while my mother looked expectantly at my dad, eyebrows raised.

"Hello?" I mumbled around the mouthful of food.

"You're to come at 0600 and 1700, sharp. You can clean up the backyard, do the litter box, and walk Poco. I'll feed and water them. You forgot to bring the trash bins in. Don't let it happen again."

It was the infamous Amos ordering me around like he was Principal Black during a fire drill. I might have snapped just a tiny bit in reply.

"What makes you think I ever want to set foot anywhere near you again?" I said, not caring he was an adult.

Who did he think he was, bossing me around? My hackles must have risen visibly, because my mom signaled me to stop being so sassy. She held out her hand, and I gladly gave her the phone.

"This is Mrs. St. Claire. Gabby is delighted to be of service." She stared at me, eyebrows raised in that don't-get-in-trouble look. "She'll be there at six tomorrow morning."

I frowned, feeling even more aggravated than before.

Why couldn't anything go right in my life?

CHAPTER 14

"Gabby, you just have to keep the job." Becca's voice expressed her incredulousness. Even over the phone I could imagine my BFF's brown eyes rolling. "This could be the start of your own business. You'd become an entrepreneur just like Mr. Cicorelli talked about in class at the beginning of the year."

I lay on the floor in my room, legs on my bed so I could do crunches while Becca played devil's advocate. Only my BFF would remember what we covered during the first month of school. I proceeded to give my final but weakest argument against continuing as a professional pet sitter.

"They won't be back for another week, and I have to get up an hour earlier every day so I can walk the dog before I go to school. Do you have any idea how dark it is at 5:30 a.m.?"

"Yes, I do. I routinely get up that early," Becca said.

I had been expecting that answer and was ready with my own comeback. "Then you know how badly it would suck. Plus, the crazy guy." I couldn't understand why a cop's kid, of all people, would dismiss the whack factor so quickly. "He might be a serial killer or something."

Note to self: Stop saying "serial killer." I was afraid that if I said it often enough, in some strange twist of fate I might actually meet one.

"You have too much imagination, Gabby. If you take this job, you will make enough money to buy a decent bike. That means on future jobs you would not have to get up as early because you can get around more quickly. A bike would not only be a capital resource, it would provide recreational opportunities for both of us this summer."

I skipped over the capital resource thing, whatever that meant, and considered the summer possibilities. Bikes would certainly expand the number of places I could go, since at almost fourteen, I was not going to be driving anytime soon.

"Tootsie, don't forget the dishes," my mom called as she walked by my bedroom door.

"True," I conceded while hauling myself

upright and downstairs. "But unless Pete's parents fixed or got him a bike, it's not like I'd be hanging out with him more."

I cradled the phone between my ear and shoulder as I started filling the sink, thinking for the zillionth time it would be nice if we had a mechanical dishwasher like everyone else.

"About this Pete thing," Becca began.

I cringed. I hated it when she sounded like a parent and even more when she turned out to be right. But I didn't want to get in another argument with her, so I derailed her train of thought.

"Yeah, even if the Pete thing fizzles out, the two of us would ride together," I inserted quickly as I loaded dirty dishes into the hot, soapy water. The lemony smell was a welcome distraction from the usual stale cigarette odor that lingered on my dad's coat after a night out with the guys. "Plus, I'd rather pet sit than help Mom clean this summer. Remember last time at the Diva's? The sleepover and the notes in the trash?"

My mom had suggested I spend part of my summer helping her clean houses, but after the disaster at Donabell Bullock's a month ago, when I'd been publically humiliated in front of half the seventh grade, I had not been too keen on taking my mom up on the offer.

"Gabby, Pete may just be using you as part of his cover-up. What better way to divert suspicion off of himself than to spend all this time, with a witness, looking for the lost dog?"

"Pete wouldn't do that!"

"He has motive—his jealousy of Lana. He had means to get inside—credit card."

"Three dogs are missing." I scrubbed the potato pot extra hard.

"Maybe he let the other two dogs loose by accident."

"Pete couldn't have done it," I said with more conviction than I felt. "How could he be at Oceanside Boarding and be at Lana's dance recital out of town?"

Having said it, I felt my confidence in Pete's innocence rise 100 percent.

"Find out when they got home, when they went to pick up Fluffnstuff, and if there was enough time in between for him to get there from home and back."

Like I said, I hated it when Becca talked like this.

Dear Watson,

I have these ginormous decisions to make, facts to find, and pets to sit. Not that pet sitting is simple, because of this freaky guy who gives me the creeps. And I may have a boyfriend who wants to be a hero, but Becca thinks he might actually be a creep.

So I have to figure out what really happened to the missing dogs in order to clear Pete, and then I can have my happily ever after.

Right?

CHAPTER 15

Lunch Monday was almost as good as being on stage. The entire table was wide eyed at my dangerous pet-sitting encounter, especially when I got to the human handcuff part. When I got to the tattoo part, Brandon interrupted.

"Navy SEAL," he insisted. "The tattoo gives it away. Those guys are rad."

The admiration in his voice surprised me. I figured he missed the whole vagrant description, so I repeated it. "He looked like he lived in a cardboard box with his scraggly, long hair and beard. If he was navy, he'd have a buzz cut."

Living in an area with army, navy, and air stations, I'd seen enough military guys to know.

"No, SEALs look like that on purpose, kind of a disguise like a cop going undercover wears. They do secret missions and everything. My dad said Navy SEALs jump out of planes at night, land in the ocean, swim ten, twenty miles to an enemy ship or outpost, and blow it up."

He was evidently impressed, but it sounded more like mythology to me.

"I bet he looked buff, didn't he?" Brandon asked.

I had to think about it. I had pretty much focused on the bum leg, but I vaguely recalled the other one looking strong and muscly. I hadn't seen him again, but I had heard noise upstairs that sounded like weights, big, heavy weights, thumping down on the floor.

"You said he had a steely grip," Becca reminded me.

"There's a movie coming out about SEALs," Pete volunteered. He wore a T-shirt under a button-down long-sleeved shirt left deliberately unbuttoned halfway so the shirt showed. Just like Clark Kent when he morphed into Superman.

Clever fashion statement.

"We ought to catch it sometime." He looked right at me when he said it.

Is he asking me out?

I needed a second opinion. I shot a quick glance at Becca, but she was staring at Brandon. Why? Because he was her crush, or because she was deliberately ignoring this whole exchange?

How were we going to decipher it later if she didn't pay attention to the details?

I banged her knee under the table with mine.

"Not this week," Brandon said. "I have a dance competition soon and need to focus."

Pete nodded but was still looking at me. I choked down the peanut butter that seemed intent on sticking to my tongue.

"Sounds like a plan," I finally managed.

Pete broke into a grin. Heat rose on my face, and I hoped it didn't show like some neon sign advertising what a dorkina I was. I tapped Becca under the table with my foot, but she still pretended not to notice. I took a long swig from my juice box to hide my displeasure.

Maybe all those teen magazines were right. Having a BF messes up all your other important relationships.

CHAPTER 16

In Civics and Economics, probably the most stupid, boring class ever, Mr. Cicorelli droned on and on about people making choices and these choices having costs. He probably could bore an insomniac to sleep with his dreary, nasal voice.

"*Opportunity cost* is defined as the next-best alternative not chosen, or the alternative given up, when we make a decision," he said.

Had Pete said something about opportunity cost? I racked my brain to remember but came up empty. I decided I better tune in because, if Pete mentioned it, it might be important in our relationship.

"There are opportunity costs in making decisions about which TV show you watch at a certain time, how to spend your allowance, or what to wear to school," Mr. C. said. "I need a volunteer to tell us about a choice they made, what they gave up, and if they were happy with that choice. Who has an example?"

I didn't bother raising my hand because the Diva had raised hers, glancing around with frosty eyes, daring someone to be foolish enough to compete for the teacher's attention.

"Donabell, give us your example." Mr. C. smiled encouragingly. Not that the Diva needed any.

"Last time I had my hair done, I chose a demure highlight that would accentuate the natural beauty of my hair rather than some gaudy color that screamed 'notice me!'"

Orange Hair visibly sank lower into her seat. Her face flamed red, grotesquely clashing with her pumpkin-colored hair.

"Great example, Donabell." His praise made her preen like a peacock.

He had no clue the Diva had used his question to put a new student in her place. It seemed like Orange Hair got the not-so-subtle message, because she cringed like a kicked puppy.

"All economic questions and problems arise from scarcity," he said. "Economics assumes people do not have the resources to satisfy all of their wants. Therefore, we must make choices about how to allocate those resources. We make decisions about how to spend our money and use our time."

I had no idea why seventh graders needed to know this stuff or the four functions of the Federal Reserve Bank. Most of us probably banked in Mason jars or sock drawers, or not at all.

"Please make sure you have a firm understanding of the concept of opportunity cost so your homework is done correctly. Divide a page in your notebook into two columns, with one column labeled 'choice' and the other 'opportunity cost.' List at least five choices you make today and the corresponding opportunity cost for those choices. We'll be using those lists in class tomorrow before handing them in. Use the remainder of class to work with a shoulder partner to start your lists."

As usual, the Devotees (the Diva's inner circle of suck-up friends) gazed at her, begging with their eyes, "Choose me! Choose me." I could have barfed. The people around me paired up, leaving me and Orange Hair to work together.

I sighed. It could have been worse. I could have been stuck with the Diva.

CHAPTER 17

Taco Tuesday only happened once a month, so the extra-long lunch line stretched around the OMS cafeteria like Mr. Fantastic's arms. Students were extra loud and antsy, with more than the usual cutting in line because of the menu.

Becca and I sat in stony muteness, waiting for our BFFLs. I switched to bringing my lunch in fifth grade when Dad started "borrowing" my lunch money. I figured it was one small way I could contribute to Dad's sobriety. Becca routinely brought her lunch because her parents were health-food nuts. They probably classified tacos with arsenic and Twinkies.

As the silence between us continued, I resolved that I wasn't going to be the first one to speak. She was the one who acted like a jerk at lunch yesterday and then never bothered to call last night and apologize. I would wait her out. Even if the tension was building like a tidal wave.

Tick. Tick. Tick. I tried staring.

Becca never looked up.

Tick. Tick. Tick. I scooted my chair back loudly.

No reaction.

Tick. Tick. Tick. I slurped my drink.

Nothing.

A wave of relief swept over me as Pete, Brandon, and Paulette dropped their trays down. An unexpected fourth tray hit the table.

I glanced up to see a strange girl with blonde bobbed hair pulling out a seat across from Paulette. It was Orange Hair. Except now it was an uneven blonde. Definitely a home job.

"Hi, I'm Wanda, Gabby's partner in Econ," she said with forced cheerfulness and a fragile smile.

I could have mentioned the partnership was a one-time thing and that didn't entitle her to invite herself into my BFFL group, but I kind of felt sorry for her. The Diva's comment about her orange hair had probably shamed her into dyeing it the moment she got home. Plus, she'd mentioned something to me in class yesterday about her parents being divorced and how hard it was to be the new girl.

"Hey," Pete mumbled around a mouthful of taco. Today his hair had been gelled into little spikes in front. He had on a faded black hoodie with Captain America and Thor half washed away.

"Wassup?" Brandon nodded in recognition and inhaled two-thirds of a taco.

Wanda plopped herself into the seat. Her shoulders dropped as some of the tension in them faded away. Maybe she was just looking for a place to belong.

I pulled out an apple before addressing my BFFLs. "So, I got a bike last night," I said super casually.

Out of the corner of my eye I watched for Pete's reaction. I wanted him to be thrilled and suggest spending our lives together, pedaling down the ribbon of road we called life into a glorious sunset, the lyrics of *People Will Say We're in Love* playing softly in the background.

He gave me a thumbs-up with the hand not shoveling another taco in his mouth.

"Where?" asked Becca, with ice framing the word.

I maintained my composure but inwardly smirked that she'd spoken to me first. "Short version is I got a deal on my wheels."

The long version went something like this:

Last night, Amos had stopped pumping iron long enough to give me $110.00, claiming the extra $2.00 was a tip from Poco. I figured it was from his guilty conscience for scaring me to death, then almost getting me fired. When I showed my mom what I'd earned, she hustled me right out the door to a thrift store two doors down from where she worked.

A skinny Goth girl had greeted my mom by name, making me think my mom came here often. The employee pulled out a beat-up, fat-tired mountain bike that had been blue at one time, but now looked like someone had sandpapered off most of the paint and dragged it through the Great Dismal Swamp, in case it wasn't ugly enough.

Goth Girl had insisted it was one sturdy bike, a great buy at only seventy dollars.

Before I realized what was happening, my mom had said we'd take it, I'd paid, and then we were out the door.

I had to admit, after trying it out, that the bike rode well. Now all I needed was a riding buddy. Somebody blond and . . .

"You should have waited for the police auction," Becca commented with a snit in her voice.

"Well—" I started.

But Becca continued. "By the way, my dad said the missing Irish setter was found at the Virginia Beach Animal Control. He was reunited with his owners last night." She paused, then added, "That's in case anyone here still cares about missing dogs."

Thanks a million, Becca. Brush my big news aside with a thinly veiled slam on my BF. Have you been taking lessons from the Diva?

"That's great!" Bran said.

Just like flipping a light switch, Becca turned on a smile.

"I would just die if someone kidnapped Puddles or Mr. Jangles." A touch of fear stained Paulette's voice.

"Are they dogs?" asked Wanda.

"Puddles is. Mr. Jangles is my horse."

"You have a horse?" Wanda's mouth opened. Good thing she hadn't started scarfing down her final taco yet. It would have been see-food gross. "Wow."

"Mr. Jangles isn't likely to go missing since horse rustling went out with the Wild West, stagecoaches, and cowboys," Becca said with her mother's ask-a-stupid-question tone. "However, dognapping is alive and well on the East Coast, so maybe you ought to make your dog less of a target by keeping her at home."

"I do," said Paulette. "I don't board her, ever. She even sleeps in my room."

"Does she still wear that ruby collar that matches your bracelet?" Becca's voice contained more than a touch of annoyance.

"Yes," Paulette said timidly. She held up her left hand. Even in the harsh cafeteria light it sparkled like liquid fire encircling her wrist.

"Wow," said Wanda with admiration. "Nice bling."

"It's not bling," Paulette corrected. "It's the real deal, as Daddy says. He got it for me on my thirteenth birthday, and it has one ruby for each year that I am old."

I didn't know how much rubies cost, but my mom had gotten $200 when she pawned her engagement ring to bail Dad out after he got a DUI. I wasn't supposed to know about the arrest or the pawnshop. But after overhearing Mom talking to some lawyer, I had snooped around.

The diamond in Mom's ring was smaller than any of the rubies in Paulette's bracelet. I was no math genius, but even I could figure out that if pawnshops paid maybe 50 percent of an item's value, Paulette was walking around with at least five grand on her arm. Wanda must have been doing the math as well.

"Does the dog's collar have thirteen real rubies, too?" She reached out to touch the bracelet.

"Yes, except her collar is leather, not gold," Paulette said.

Gold. I hadn't figured in the cost of real gold. Her bracelet was probably worth two of our vans, with my bike thrown in to pay the tax.

Noise from the Mocha Loco table caught my attention. I glanced over, hoping none of them were noticing this display. No such luck. One of the younger toadies leaned toward Raff, talking and pointing in our direction. I quickly grabbed Paulette's arm and pulled it down. No sense drawing the attention of that crowd.

After *Oklahoma* I had taken Paulette under my protective wing. Sure, she had money and looks, but she was a few puppies short of a pet shop in the brain department. How in the world she'd managed not to have such an expensive bracelet stolen was beyond me.

"Do Puddles a favor and get her a plain collar from Walmart," Becca told her. "You'd hate to have someone dognap and ransom her like they did Elizabeth Barrett Browning's dog."

"Oh no. Poor Elizabeth. I didn't know her dog was stolen." Sincere worry etched Paulette's voice. "Is she the eighth grader with braces in chorus?"

"Don't be ridiculous," Becca snapped. "Browning was a famous, dead poet we read about last year." Her tone drew everyone's attention at the table. "I just used her as an example because, even if my dad had named names of local people and recent cases of people holding a pet for a ransom, I wouldn't dish." She stared straight at me when she added, "I can keep a secret."

She snorted, stood, and grabbed her trash, shoving it into her nearly new brown bag. I watched in disbelief as she stormed off to deposit it in the trash.

Becca never, ever threw away her brown bags until they had so many holes and tears they resembled tattered tan rags. That was another weird thing about her family. The Chapmans recycled everything, including the Sunday comics, which they used as gift wrap. They even reused bubble wrap. What kind of freak parents forbid their kids to pinch bubble wrap so they can reuse it?

Something was seriously amiss for Becca to trash her bag. And what was she implying about keeping a secret? I hadn't blabbered anything. Was she just acting like she had inside info? I glanced over and noticed Paulette's bottom lip quivering, tears starting to well.

"I dunno," I said, shrugging. "It's not like hot sauce set her off."

It was a lame attempt at humor and fell flat. Becca was nice to everyone. For her to snap at someone kind of defenseless like Paulette worried me.

Everyone nodded and got back to either eating or making small talk.

Pete leaned toward me. "Now that you have a bike, what do you say we head over to Animal Control after school? Unless you have other plans."

"No. I mean, yes. I mean, no, I don't have other plans, but yes, I can," I said, wishing once again I could press rewind and start again.

Brandon pretended to be engrossed in his fifth taco, but I could see he was holding in a smile.

I wondered if he knew about Pete and me and Saturday. I wondered if he and Pete had talked all about it like Becca and I had. If they had discussed it, I doubted Brandon had read him the riot act and warned him away from me.

Tonight Watson and I were going to have a chat.

Dear Watson,

Does "opportunity cost" mean giving up a best friend when a boyfriend comes along?

CHAPTER 18

"Sweet ride," Pete said.

His sleeve touched mine, and I fumbled with my bike lock.

"Pet sitting must be good money," he continued.

"I can't complain." It took three tries before I wrestled off the lock. Finally, I climbed on my new bike. "I thought after we hit Animal Control we might swing by Paws and Furballs. They aren't all that far from each other."

"Good excuses to glide the ride?" Pete joked as he swung onto his blue mountain bike.

The chill March wind was at our backs, subtly pushing us away from school while running its icy fingers under my jacket. Pete's comment had presented me with a dilemma. Although this trip wasn't about my ride, it wasn't exactly about missing dogs either. Did that make it a date? More disturbing: Did that make me a hypocrite because I was acting like it was about the dogs when really I just wanted to hang out with Pete?

We coasted into Animal Control, a bleak off-white building with fences on the left side and out back. Someone had painted large murals of cats, dogs, birds, and a couple of rabbits on one side, but it must have been ages ago, since the paint was faded, peeling, or missing in splotches. Muffled barking emanated from inside. Pete used his cable lock to secure both of our bikes after we parked.

I was glad he was bent down so he didn't see the stupid smile plastered across my face. I couldn't help it. It seemed gallant and all, but it was almost a symbolic experience: our bikes, joined together. Like Pete and me. I had to pretend to brush my hair out of my eyes when he stood to face me so he didn't see me grinning like the village idiot.

He held out his hand. My heart skipped a beat, but I took it. He interlaced his fingers in mine, and we headed inside. Together. For once I was happy about the awful weather. My hands would not perspire in this cold.

It went downhill from there.

Apparently, the police had already asked Animal Control to be on the lookout for the two dogs still missing: Fluffnstuff and some guy's pit bull. The harried counter clerk treated Pete and me like bothersome toddlers, barely making eye contact and answering in a clipped, annoyed tone. Pete and I exchanged glances, rolled our eyes, and left.

We hadn't pedaled out of the parking lot before Pete's chain fell off. I tried to help as he fiddled with it, but words like *sprocket, cog, crank set,* and *bike cassettes* were all lost on me. I got grease on my hands, jeans, jacket, and even in my hair because the wind kept whipping my frizzy locks into my eyes.

"I'm gonna have to call someone to come get me," Pete grumbled. "Not to keep complaining, but I've told Dad like a bazillion times that I need a new crank set 'cuz this one is too worn to hold the chain. But he can't take a couple of minutes to take me to the store and help me put it on. It's always 'after Lana's this' and 'maybe if Lana that.'"

We walked back inside, Pete not offering to hold hands. I tried to decide if it was because of the grease or his mood or if I had done something wrong. The grouchy lady at the counter ordered Pete into the restroom to wash his hands before she'd let him touch the phone.

I glanced at the clock—4:15. I'd have to be at Wrangleys' no later than 5:00. While Pete called his dad, I tried to clean up in the restroom that smelled of mildew and old papers. Glancing in the grubby mirror, I was horrified to find grease smeared under one eye and on my cheek. I looked like a half-raccoon mutant. After some painful scrubbing, the grease came off only to be replaced with cherry-red splotches.

"Dad's gonna swing by *after* he picks up Lana," Pete said with a sigh. "Since her tap class ends at 5:00 p.m., it's gonna be dark by the time he gets here."

I have to tell him I can't wait. I have to pet sit! said my brain.

I can't desert him, not now. He might break up with me, said my heart.

As the voices in my head warred back and forth, stupid Mr. C.'s voice chimed in with "*Opportunity cost* is giving up the second-best alternative to obtain something else." In my mind's eye I grabbed a remote control and switched him off. There had to be a way to keep both job and boyfriend.

"Pete, Pocococo's—" I started.

Pete grabbed my arm and pointed at a white van with Pollack Laboratories emblazoned on the side. Instead of parking, the vehicle pulled around to the back of the building.

Our eyes met. We nodded and ever so casually made our way around the side of the building, hugging the wall. The van disappeared around the final corner. Like spies, we scuttled to the edge of the building, squatted low, and peered carefully around the bend.

I was aware of Pete's hand resting on my back, his minty breath, and the tension that surrounded us.

The van backed up to the service door, and a man in white coveralls hopped out from the driver's side. He rapped on the back door and, without waiting for a response, opened the back doors on the van. The building door opened, and Mrs. Harried Clerk came out pulling a German shepherd on a short leash.

Pete and I stared at each other, and then back at the scene unfolding. I was sure we were thinking the same thing. People's pets were being forked over for testing purposes. I wondered if purebred animals were somehow better to experiment on.

Harried Clerk went inside, and the man forced the dog inside the back of the van, closing the doors with a clang that sounded like prison doors slamming shut. He hopped back in the still-running van and pulled away.

Right toward us.

We scrambled up and dashed toward the front. The van was too quick. We'd been spotted.

"They're closing now," called the driver through his half-mast driver's side window.

I was momentarily speechless but managed to wave weakly. Pete did that guy head-jerk thing, hands casually stuffed in his pockets like the side of Animal Control was a regular gathering place for teens.

I doubted we fooled the guy. He knew we'd seen whatever had gone down. Fortunately, he kept on driving rather than eliminating us witnesses on the spot.

"Maybe we should report this." Pete raised his eyebrows. "Do you think?"

"Maybe. I mean, he came after hours to the back door. But who do we report it to?"

Pete shrugged. "I dunno. Becca's dad is a cop, right? Ask her."

I briefly thought about telling him Becca and I weren't exactly on speaking terms, but that might lead to talking about stuff like Becca thinking Pete was mixed up in the dogs' disappearance. I decided to play it safe and postpone that conversation until I'd thought more about it.

"Pete, I gotta go pet sit. But I don't want to leave you here alone in case the van guy comes back."

Pete stared at me like I'd spoken in Martian.

"In case he comes back to get rid of witnesses," I clarified.

Pete laughed and squeezed my hand. "I can take of myself, but you go on. I'll call you if anything else happens."

I wanted to point out that if anything happened to him, like being maced and kidnapped in the back of a dog-stealing drug company van, or if Harried Clerk unleashed the proverbial hounds to tear him to shreds, he'd be unable to call me. But then I recalled an article Becca and I had read in *USA Girls* about always playing along when guys acted macho.

Mr. C.'s words haunted me once again as I pedaled out of the parking lot. Apparently the opportunity cost of stroking a guy's ego was letting him get killed by dognapping goons.

CHAPTER 19

Not only had I been late to pet sit and gotten reprimanded by Amos the SEAL, I'd also been late to math the following day.

"Looking for another detention, Miss St. Claire?" Ms. Lynnet snapped, arms crossed and beady eyes drilling a hole in my forehead. That woman might have had it in for everyone, even Miss Goody-Two-Shoes Becca, but she particularly delighted in torturing me.

The only tolerable part of being in the Nazi-witch-queen's math class was Brandon. I was delighted when he passed me a note.

I was undelighted when I read it.

"Paulette's in tears today. I think something happened to her dog."

The bad news was confirmed at lunch.

"We were leaving Pampered Pets, where Puddles gets groomed, when this guy wearing black snatched Puddles out of my hands and took off. He kind of shoved me, and by the time

I recovered, they'd disappeared." Paulette's bottom lip quivered, and tears pooled in her already red eyes. "Daddy told the police, but he didn't think they'd find her. Please say you'll try to find Puddles when you look for Lana's dog."

She looked at Pete and me with utter desperation.

"We'll look high and low," I promised, trying to mentally connect the dots between the Irish setter that had been found in the animal shelter, the missing cocker spaniel and pit bull, and now Paulette's Yorkie. "What did this guy look like? Did you recognize him?"

"No. He had on all black and an inside-out hoodie pulled up over his head and a ski mask on his face."

This was not good. Whoever had dognapped Puddles had not wanted to be recognized and had done an excellent job of it.

"Can you remember anything else? Height? Eye color, maybe?"

"Umm, about my height. I think he had blond hair. Some of it was poking out from the eye holes."

"What color blond?" asked Brandon. "Platinum blond like yours or dirty blond like Pete's?"

"My hair's not dirty. It's gelled," Pete said. "Leave my hair out of it."

I could tell he was in a bad mood, probably from having to wait for his dad in the cold, alone and wondering if he was going to get snuffed for witnessing a criminal transaction.

"Like Pete's," answered Paulette after scrutinizing my boyfriend's face.

"Was the kid skinny or fat?" I asked.

"It's hard to say. In between, I guess." Paulette opened her notebook and pulled out several pictures of Puddles. "I thought you might need these."

The photos showed Puddles relaxing on a prissy pink comforter, Puddles and Paulette lounging on a float in a pool, Puddles dressed in an angel costume. My eyes were drawn to the collar. It was wide enough to keep Puddles's fur from blocking the display of rubies.

"Looks like your new friend has deserted us for the Cool Table," Becca said.

I turned around in my seat to see Wanda sitting at the Diva's table but on the outer edges with the wannabes. That was a change I hadn't seen coming.

I wasn't particularly fond of Wanda, but Becca was getting on my nerves. Without thinking I retorted, "Who knows, maybe you'll be joining them tomorrow."

"Trying to get rid of me? I see how it is." Becca shoved away from the table and stormed off.

"I'm sorry, Gabby. I didn't mean to make Becca mad." Paulette burst into tears.

I put my arm around her and patted her back. Pete handed her an unused napkin.

"It's not your fault." I tried rubbing her back, but she only cried harder.

Brandon and Pete both decided to bail. Brandon handed me another napkin, and Pete signed "bikes" and pointed to his watch.

I hoped that meant meet him after school at the bike rack.

While Paulette cleaned up in the restroom, I looked at the photos of Puddles again and reviewed Paulette's description of the dognapper. He was an average sort of guy with blond hair and an inside-out black hoodie. Maybe the black hoodie had some distinguishing features, like a school logo or personalized name, which had prompted the criminal to turn it inside out.

Pete had been wearing a black hoodie with Thor and Captain America just yesterday.

Pete knew about the valuable collar.

Gabby, stop this right now!

Lots of guys, like Pete, had blond hair and black hoodies. It would be ludicrous to suspect Pete, since he had been with me after school. Pete was a good guy. He wouldn't be behind these crimes, no matter what Becca had insinuated. I was 100 percent sure of that.

But I couldn't help myself.

I had to ask. Just to be sure.

"Paulette, what time did you pick Puddles up from the groomers?" I asked when she returned from the bathroom.

She sucked on her bottom lip for a moment. "I don't know exactly, because we'd had dinner at the country club, and then Mom had Daddy swung by the Harrison Opera House."

I mentally tried to figure out the timeline of events. Sometime after dinner and after swinging by a place in a neighboring city. This was not good. But maybe they'd had a really early dinner. It had been a school night, I rationalized.

I hated myself but had to ask; I had to know. "Best guess—before or after eight?"

"It was almost nine, I think."

The PB&J in my stomach formed a rock. My

knees felt weak. “Are you sure?”

Paulette shrugged and looked at me with her still red-rimmed eyes.

The realization nearly had me reeling.

Pete would have had plenty of time to get home, fix his bike, and kidnap Puddles. What if he *was* the dognapper?

CHAPTER 20

Instead of paying attention to behavioral adaptations in the Cnidarian phylum, I was worried about meeting Pete after school. What if he were the one behind these missing dogs? I needed to go over the evidence. Surely I'd find something to clear him.

Motives: the original dogs might have been taken related to competition in the marketplace (according to Becca, who may or may not be unbiased) or because someone was mad at one of the owners or because stud fees were so high or because Pollack Labs needed test animals or because Paws and Furballs was making a statement or because the moon was made of green cheese.

There were just too many options. I decided to put motive aside and check into opportunity.

Who would have opportunity to be at both Oceanside Boarding and Pampered Pets? Again, too many options.

I was getting nowhere, and now another dog was missing.

"With your group, compare and contrast your lists." Ms. Shernick's voice pulled me back to the present.

Students were scooting chairs, partnering up. I sighed. One of my group, Maria, barely spoke English and would have nothing to contribute, but I figured Hannah the Brainiac would have enough for all three of us. She did not disappoint.

"By the way, Mrs. Baker wants you to stop by after school today to talk to her," Hannah said.

She was Mrs. Baker's foster child and a mystery in her own right. I knew she'd been in court and her parents were in jail, but since I was already up to my ears in problems, I pushed that puzzle aside and tried to focus on jellyfish.

"Yeah, sure," I said. I decided to tell her what Pete and I had seen at Animal Control just to see what her reaction was.

"Figures," she said with a brittleness I'd never heard in her voice before. "Those people will do anything—test on animals, experiment on poor people in third world countries and mental patients who don't know what they are consenting to. I wouldn't be surprised at all to find out they grabbed these dogs. If they did, no one will ever see them again."

Just then Raff sauntered over to our group.

"Check it out, Maria." He stuck out his wrist so she could admire his new watch.

"Is that what I think it is?" asked Hannah. "A Rolex?"

"*Si, si, senorita*. Matches my ankle bracelet." Raff raised his foot up so we could compare the two side by side. His ankle monitoring bracelet was his pride and joy.

"Focus, people! Focus!" Ms. Shernick clapped her hands and scanned the class to see who was and wasn't deeply engrossed in the riveting lives of sea sponges.

Where did Raff get the money for a Rolex?

By stealing something, no doubt. Relief flooded my entire body. Raff must have kidnapped Puddles and pawned her collar for his watch. It made sense. Raff's character was shady, he hung with the wrong group, and he prided himself in breaking the law.

And, if that was true, that meant that Pete . . . was a free man.

I couldn't wait to meet up with him after school.

CHAPTER 21

I pedaled against the wind, my hair whipping around like tiny lashes, whacking my face. It was more than annoying because the experience reminded me of my whole life: fighting against the wind, being beaten down by problems, swimming upstream. No matter what I did right, fifty bazillion other things would jump at the chance to go wrong.

But at least it occasionally interrupted my dismal train of thought chugging away on the question track.

Did having a boyfriend mean losing a best friend? Would Pete turn out to be a good thing or a bad thing? What could I do to keep both my BFF and my BF? How does a teenager know what to do to make things turn out right?

I'd been so lost in the muddle of my thoughts that I hadn't seen the snarled stopped traffic and almost ran into Pete at the corner of Grove and Chestnut. For the fifty bazillionth time I brushed hair out of my eyes to get a better look. A mattress and box springs had spilled onto the pavement, tangling traffic.

Pete was able to balance on his bike without moving, but I hadn't mastered that yet. I bumped the car beside me. The driver pounded his fist on his window at me. I mouthed "sorry" and set one foot down to balance. We had a mile or so to go to get to Pollack Labs, and I still had no idea what we'd do once we got there.

"Gabby! Is that . . . ?"

I turned to look in the direction Pete was pointing. Two cars ahead, a Yorkie had its head stuck out of the back passenger window. The afternoon sun's rays reflected off of something gleaming around its neck.

My pulse started to race. Was it Puddles?

"We need to get closer," I yelled over the din of stopped cars.

I edged my bike around a delivery truck in front of us. The driver behind honked at me. Pete pedaled onto the sidewalk and around.

"Kid! Get out of the road!" yelled a voice.

Traffic was starting to move, so I propelled myself forward. The dog stood on its hind legs and looked out of the rear window.

I maneuvered around to the driver's side of

the dog car. It was an older- model gray, a four door. I bent low. Someone pulled the dog into the front seat but not before I'd gotten a definitive look.

A Yorkie with a ruby collar. Just like the one in Paulette's pictures.

Bingo.

We had our culprit.

CHAPTER 22

Had being the operative word.

The driver gunned the engine, and the gray car lurched onto Chestnut. Pete and I did our best to tail him, but between traffic and getting separated, it was a lost cause. I spent the next twenty minutes fruitlessly cruising streets that got less inhabited, dingier, and dirtier the further I went, hoping either the gray car or Pete would turn up.

Instead Raff turned up.

I had just turned out of an alley onto a side street when I saw him napping in a rusty folding chair, tipped way back to lean against the front of a seedy store. The lot next to the store was vacant except for empty plastic bags and fast food trash. The rest of the street seemed deserted of people, even though parked cars and a battered van lined either side.

Lying next to Raff, its leash looped under a back chair leg, was a pit bull. I froze, wondering if the dog would tear into me, wondering how badly Raff would be injured when the dog yanked the leash and toppled my classmate onto the cracked cement walk.

Flashing pink neon lights proclaiming Paradise Pawn splashed across the mostly white pit bull, making him look like someone had run him through the wash with red clothes. Raff's hands were stuffed in the pockets of his leather jacket, head in a hoodie with wires coming out and disappearing into a pocket. I hoped both he and the dog were asleep or so into the music they'd never even know I was there.

I glanced around, hoping Pete would materialize. Joe's Pool Hall. A washateria. A tattoo parlor. An ABC liquor store. A couple of other dull brick three stories. The pit bull and Raff might fit right in, but I was feeling as conspicuous as I would have at a formal dinner at the White House.

Pit bull? Could this be the missing pit bull? From the corner of my eye I noticed movement. I jerked my head right and felt relief wash through me like a cold slushie as Pete rounded a corner and pulled up next to me.

"Got 'em?" I asked.

He shook his head. "I lost 'em."

"Me too."

The pawnshop door opened and a figure in black, complete with sunglasses and a hoodie up over his ears, stepped out and started up the street. The pit bull followed the figure with his eyes, but Raff seemed blissfully unaware.

"What do we do now?" I asked, hoping Pete had an idea.

A car engine started up. The hooded figure cut in front of the rusted van and disappeared.

"I dunno. Do you think we have time to still go by the lab?" As Pete spoke, a car in front of the rusty van pulled into the street and roared away, coughing dark smoke from its tailpipe. It was gray, with a small dog in the back.

Pete and I exchanged a hurried glance as we sprinted on our bikes after it. We closed in. The Yorkie jumped up and down in the backseat. It was easy to see the collar was gone.

Then an all-too-familiar sound tormented me. The sound of Pete's bike chain coming off.

CHAPTER 23

Dear Watson,

News on the case thus far:

Irish setter found.

Paulette's dog kidnapped by guy in black with blond hair and a gray car driven by an accomplice.

Pollack Labs truck picked up German shepherd at Animal Control, after hours from the back. Pete was with me and could not have been involved.

I read over my entry and realized I was trying to prove Pete innocent more than I was relating the facts of the puzzling mystery.

Stick to the facts, Sherlock.

Great. Not only was I talking to a diary, it had started talking back. Was I going nuts?

I pushed investigating my sanity or lack thereof to a back burner and concentrated on the matter at hand. I steeled myself to be objective and started writing again.

Fact: Paulette's dog missing, seen with collar on, then missing collar within minutes. Possible clues near Paradise Pawn.

Raff: Rolex watch, pit bull, Paradise Pawn.

The phone rang. I glanced at my clock radio: 7:45.

Must be Becca has finally come to her senses. A weight lifted from my soul.

"Telephone, Gabby," my dad called.

I raced downstairs, picked up the phone, and slowed down so I didn't sound out of breath and too eager. Becca still owed me an apology. I'd forgive her, but I wouldn't grovel like the Diva's Devotees did.

"Guess who turned up?" Pete sounded excited.

I mentally shifted gears to talk to my boyfriend. "Fluffnstuff?"

"Yup. Get this—someone turned him in to a Hampton shelter." Hampton was a city about twenty miles away and accessible only through a series of bridges and tunnels. No way Fluff could have gotten to Hampton without human help. And no way Pete could have been the human help. Besides, I'd seen another figure wearing a black sweatshirt disappear into that gray car.

On the inside I was doing my happy dance. Pete was in the clear!

"Guess who drove me to the Cycle Shop while Mom and Lana went to Hampton?"

"Your dad?"

"Yup. And instead of just fixing my old bike, he bought me a brand-new 820. Of course I had to pitch in some cash, but it's worth it."

Pete described the bike, going into detail just like Becca did about Brandon, but even after his report I couldn't have identified an 820 from a UFO. I said "great" and "wow" in all the right places but remained clueless about "hardtail," "two-niners," and "full suspension."

"So, what do you say we catch a movie this weekend? Celebrate finding Fluff and our one-week anniversary."

I was so caught off guard, I sank to the floor. I couldn't speak.

Our one-week anniversary! You had to have a boyfriend to have an anniversary. That meant I was *for sure* for sure somebody's girlfriend. I wanted to break into my happy dance for real, but it was hard to do collapsed on the floor.

"Ya-uh." A half squeak, half grunt emanated

from my lips, and I squeezed my eyes shut at the absolute horror of it. I took a deep breath and tried again. "I'd love to."

It still came out too high and too giggly girly-girl, but at least it resembled human speech.

"I thought we'd see *Navy SEALs*, 'cuz of your Navy SEAL. It's at the mall at three. We could meet up at two and ride over?"

"Okay." The words barely pushed past the loud throbbing of my pulse slamming against my ear, beating like a bass drum on steroids.

"Great. See ya at lunch."

I sat stunned, sprawled in the hall for several minutes, soaking in the enormity of the situation.

I had a boyfriend. We had an anniversary. I was going on a date. A real date!

I started dialing Becca to share my good news, but stopped after four digits. I got up and peered at the kitchen clock.

Two minutes before eight. I had two minutes before the Chapmans' calling-in deadline. I started and stopped again. Becca might try to talk me out of going because she suspected Pete might be behind all of this.

But did she really suspect or was she just jealous? I headed back to my room, letting the minutes slide by until it was too late to call.

CHAPTER 24

"You forgot to see Mrs. Baker."

Hannah's accusing words reached through the noise and my daydream to pull me back to the OMS cafeteria.

On Fridays it was extra noisy as people made and bragged about their weekend plans. I had been waiting ever so patiently for Becca to arrive so I could do just that. I had a date to brag about.

"You better see her during lunch so you don't space it out again," Hannah continued. "It's about Pixie, her dog, and it is important."

"Has he been kidnapped?" My senses immediately went on full alert.

"No, but *she* is pregnant," Hannah explained impatiently. "She needs a pet sitter Saturday, and for some reason Mrs. Baker thinks she should hire you."

Hannah shook her head and moved away toward the Troll Table.

Mrs. Baker was an eighth-grade teacher who

directed our last play, *Oklahoma,* in which I had a starring role. As starring as an extra without lines could be. But since I kind of saved the play when I uncovered a plot to shut it down, I figured I was the star detective of the show.

I had no idea how Mrs. Baker knew that besides being the next female lead she'd cast in a play, I was also a professional pet sitter.

But now wasn't the best time to talk to her.

I glanced at the lines of full trays inching their way from the milk pit to the cashier. None of my BFFLs had emerged from the lunch-lady lineup, so I figured that since the line was crawling, I could make it to Mrs. Baker's room and back in time to brag. Cramming the remainder of my PB&J into my mouth, I hustled out of the chow hall, leaving my juice and apple to save my seat.

Not that students were lined up to sit at our table or anything.

"Gabby, thanks for stopping by," Mrs. Baker said when I walked into her classroom. "I was hoping you'd be interested in pet sitting for Pixie."

I half nodded, half shrugged. "Sure."

"Normally I'd leave her in the yard, but because we're supposed to get rain and she is very close to having the puppies, I'd rather have her inside. We've cleared out the laundry room and set up a whelping box," Mrs. Baker explained as she worked a key off her key ring.

I nodded knowledgeably, hoping to hurry her along. I had no idea what "whelping box" meant, but I could figure it out when I saw it.

"There's an old toolshed in the back. Pixie loves to get under it. She's dug out a depression so she has a cool, shady place to chill, but rain turns her special spot into a doggy mud bath. Since it will probably rain Saturday, the last thing I want is for her to get under the shed."

I was trying not to rock back and forth from foot to foot, but my impatience to return to lunch and brag was overwhelming.

Mrs. Baker must have noticed. "Do you need to use the restroom and come back for the rest of the instructions?"

"No. Go on." I steeled myself to hold still and look attentive.

"Dogs often give birth at night, when it's dark and quiet, so leave all the lights off so Pixie is comfortable." Mrs. Baker handed me the key. "I'll have her food out. Make sure she has plenty of water, but don't be alarmed if she doesn't eat much. That happens just before dogs give birth."

"Got it," I said, moving towards the door.

But Mrs. Baker wasn't done.

"Please take her out on a leash when you give her a potty break. I don't want her scooting under the shed, which I think is her preferred place for the whelping."

"I'll use the leash," I promised.

"Like I said, if she's not eating, it's a sign the puppies are coming. If the puppies do come, give her lots of space. Momma dogs can be quite . . ." Mrs. Baker searched for an appropriate word. "Aggressive. I don't think Pixie would bite under normal circumstances, but with puppies and her not knowing you, I don't want you to take any chances."

"I'll keep my distance," I promised, trying not to bolt for the door.

According to the clock I had seven minutes of lunch left. That should be enough to share the news, but since Pete would already be at the table and I couldn't just blurt it out, I'd have to come up with some clever way to drop my bomb.

"We should be back by eight Saturday night, so three visits will be plenty, morning, noon, and evening."

I smiled and nodded, hoping to save time by

stifling a verbal response.

"Is five dollars a visit enough?" Mrs. Baker cocked her head to one side, waiting for an answer.

I hadn't thought about it. I figured there was some standard price, like the seven per visit I was getting from the Wrangleys. Apparently not. I would have agreed anyway since Mrs. Baker was cool and since she was going to give me some fabulous part in the summer drama program and all.

In the interest of time, all I said was "Great."

I had almost gotten out the door when a "Gabby!" stopped me in my tracks.

Mrs. Baker.

Again.

Probably another two million rules and tips.

I turned but stayed in the doorway. Every second saved was precious.

"You need my address." Mrs. Baker scribbled on a slip of paper. "If, for some reason, we can't make it back Saturday, you could come Sunday, right?"

"Yes."

"I'll need your phone number, just in case."

I went back in and waited while she scrounged around stacks of paper on her desk for a battered day timer.

I arrived back just in time to see Paulette, Brandon, and the adorable Pete wearing his favorite Superman T, tossing their trash. Pete locked eyes with me. He looked hurt. My stomach knotted up.

"Hey, guys. I had to talk to Mrs. Baker about pet sitting her dog tomorrow." I forced myself to sound cheerful and natural. "She talked for-ev-er."

"Pete thought you'd stood us up, but I pointed out your apple and juice were on the table even if you weren't," Paulette said.

"Where's Becca?" I asked, noting her absence from our group.

"Becca sat with the nerds today, and I thought, maybe you were, like, avoiding me, us, or something too," Pete said.

"I thought maybe you missed lunch because you were looking for Puddles," Paulette said hopefully.

In my excitement about my date, I had utterly and completely forgotten about telling Paulette about seeing Puddles yesterday.

"I told her about yesterday," Pete said, still sounding wounded.

Then it struck me—so far today all I had

thought about was me.

No wonder Becca had switched tables. No wonder Pete thought whatever Pete thought. I had spent last night and today thinking about me and my big first date. Was I becoming as self-centered as the Diva?

I, Gabby St. Claire, am the worst friend in the world.

"So, is this job going to interfere with us going to the movies?" Pete's voice sounded raw.

"No. No way," I quickly assured him, hoping I was correct. I realized too late I should have figured that out before accepting the job and the key. "We're still on."

Pete visibly relaxed.

"You guys are still going to find Puddles, right?" Paulette asked.

The bell ending lunch rang, and for once, I was totally thrilled to go to class. I needed time to sort all this stuff out.

CHAPTER 25

The whole lunch thing made me realize not only that I was selfish, but also that I needed to manage my time more wisely.

I hadn't timed anything right, from chasing down gray cars to lunch to finding time for everything. Since the lecture in Econ sounded boring, I decided to invest my time by making a list of everything I had to do Saturday and any potential conflicts.

Morning: Pocococo & Pixie

Problem: How close were they? I fervently hoped they weren't on opposite sides of Virginia Beach. I looked at the address Mrs. Baker gave me, hoping I might recognize it. Relief flooded me. The two locations were practically in each other's backyards.

Noon: Pixie

Two: Meet Pete

Five: Pocococo & Pixie

I felt my whole body relax. I hadn't bitten off

more than I could chew, as my mom liked to say. Of course, it didn't leave much time to look for Puddles.

"What are some things you have to choose between, Gabby?"

The teacher's voice caught me unawares, and I knew exactly how a fawn caught in the headlights of oncoming traffic felt. I was on the verge of panic when it dawned on me that I could actually answer the question and get my brag on.

"This weekend I have two paying jobs, and"—I paused for effect like any Academy Award–winning actress would do before dropping a bombshell line—"a date, so I can't do a third thing I'd hoped to do."

I smirked at the Diva, who was giving me the customary stink eye.

"What do you know," muttered Amy Snyder, a major suck-up Devotee, "Bigfoot must have taken pity on her."

The titters of laughter from the Devotees would normally have cut like miniature knives, but not today. Today, I was armored up and ready for any trash talk they threw my way.

"Donabell?" Mr. C., oblivious to the drama that had just unfolded, had moved on.

"I thought I was going to have to choose between doing makeovers or making jewelry at my sleepover this weekend, but because of my new friend Wanda, I can do both. Wanda's uncle owns a store that sells jewelry, and Wanda's going to bring stuff so we can do both."

The Diva had outbragged me. I scowled at her smirking face. Two rows back, Wanda glowed like a radioactive isotope at being publicly acknowledged as one of the select few who'd be at the Diva's sleepover.

I did a double take. She was dressed in the same expensive name-brand styles as the Diva. Wanda was remaking herself in the Diva's image.

Who cares? Not me. I have a date.

"But where's the opportunity cost, Donabell? For there to be an opportunity cost, the next-best alternative not chosen has to be given up when we make a decision." The nuances of middle-school politics were lost on our middle-aged, balding teacher. Somehow he thought we were actually discussing his topic *du jour*.

"That's easy," gushed the Diva. "To include Wanda, I had to uninvite one of my lesser friends."

I vaguely wondered which wannabe had

been cut so copycat Wanda could have her spot. I had no problem imagining the Diva callously uninviting someone. I'd never do that to one of my friends.

Or had I? I had promised Paulette to look for Puddles, but now that something better—a date and a paying job—had come along, was I cutting her out? Had I somehow done something like that to Becca as well?

The rest of class and during half of science, I wrestled with my schedule, trying to figure out how I could do it all, and what I was compromising to get what I wanted. I finally gave up, as nothing seemed to gel and Ms. Shernick was breaking us into our groups to do a vocabulary review. I figured since Hannah was one of my partners, it would be a good time to ask what kind of dog Pixie was. I hadn't paid close enough attention when Mrs. Baker was giving me instructions.

Big mistake. Hannah went into great detail about how Pixie had once been a racing greyhound, but when she turned up pregnant, she couldn't race, and something about how Mrs. Baker didn't want her to be shot and rescued her. That part got fuzzy, since Hannah had a lot of commentary about the evils of dog racing and any kind of gambling in general, and I was tuning her out when something she mentioned grabbed my attention.

"Especially since Mr. Baker was a navy helicopter pilot before dying in a crash."

I blinked in surprise. That made Mrs. Baker some kind of war widow. This new information was like heavy-duty stuff.

Before I could ask questions, the final bell of the day and week rang. Lethargic, sleepy students came to life and burst from their seats like frenzied bees from a hive. I quickly grabbed my gear and joined the throng.

During the Friday Freedom Rush, individuals were pushed along like a piece of driftwood or an old bottle on the swelling tide of adolescent humanity, eager to start their weekend. Since the very first time I had experienced it in sixth grade, this rush had frightened me because of the disconcerting sense of powerlessness to fight the current, of being swept along without a choice.

But today, it didn't seem so scary. I felt more in control of my life than I ever had. The details, like my schedule, might be messy, but the general direction in which it was heading was finally under my control.

But by Saturday morning, everything had crashed out of control.

CHAPTER 26

On paper, my schedule had looked great: up at 5:30, Pocococo at 6:00, Bakers' at 6:45. I'd be home by 7:45 tops, with plenty of time to get ready for my movie date and do a second visit at Mrs. Baker's. After all, Pixie and Poco were mere yards apart.

What I had failed to factor in was the time it would take to go back home between the two pet-sitting jobs. I mean really, nobody *plans* to leave Mrs. Baker's key in their jeans pocket.

And how could I have known Mom would run a load of laundry for me first thing in the morning, which just happened to include the jeans with the key in the pocket? Finally, who could have foreseen that Mom would have strong objections to me earning more money?

"Mom! It's Mrs. Baker, from the play. A teacher! How can you not care I pet sit where the creepy Amos is, but be worried about me at the Bakers?"

"It is different. I know the Wrangleys, Gabby. I'm there once a week cleaning. I would know if their house was no place for a girl your age to be working."

"So, are you implying Oceanside hires axe murderers to teach eighth-grade English and direct plays?" I crossed my arms, knowing I could win this round.

"I'm just saying I want to know ahead of time where you are and who you are with. That way, if I have any doubts or questions, I can get answers *before* you get yourself into something you shouldn't have."

Her words brought a chill to my blood. I could feel the plasma freezing in my veins.

My date.

Friday night I had debated back and forth about telling Mom. I wanted to, so maybe she would help me with my hair, but I also knew Becca's parents had said she couldn't date until she was at least sixteen, and she had to be on the honor roll and a bunch of other random stuff, which basically meant she would never go out with a boy until she was ancient, like twenty-five or thirty.

So I had opted not to mention it. Just in case. I mean, it was just the movies and during the day. It wasn't like I was dating Raff or some other juvenile delinquent with a stolen Rolex that matched his ankle monitor.

"Maybe your father and I have gotten too lax about your comings and goings," my mom was saying as much to herself as me, which threw up more red flags than Beach Patrol did when a hurricane or sharks threatened the swimmers at the oceanfront.

"You're right, Mom," I quickly agreed in the most mature voice I could muster on short notice. "I should have brought it up. It's just that . . ." I paused for effect. "Mrs. Baker being a widow and single foster mom, and since you guys met her at the play, I just wasn't thinking."

"A widow? She looked awfully young to be widowed," my mom said, half-questioning and half-compassionately.

I went for the kill. "Yeah, I know, right. Navy helicopter crash. I'm sure it must have been devastating and unexpected."

I watched my mom's face soften and could tell I'd talked my way out of the jaws of disaster. This time. I allowed myself to breathe a mental sigh of relief.

"I hope you're not charging her, Gabby."

"Oh, um, well, she's the one who suggested

five dollars a visit, less than what the Wrangleys pay me."

My mom's brows knit together, so I adjusted my spiel. "But I figure when she goes to pay me, I'll tell her she doesn't have to."

"That is very thoughtful of you, Tootsie, doing it that way. Otherwise she might have felt awkward asking you to do it for free." My mom was all smiles now. "Let's find that key and get you on your way."

While making my second, unplanned morning trip to Bakers', I got behind even more because I kind of snooped at the Bakers'. It kind of was necessary because I figured I needed to check out the entire house in case Pixie decided to have her puppies somewhere other than the laundry room. I had almost convinced myself that was my sole reason for checking out the lay of Teacherland, but deep down I knew I was plain too curious for my own good.

Mrs. Baker lived in an older, two-story house. It definitely wasn't as fancy as the Wrangleys'. I looked for pictures of Mr. Baker, but there was nothing but a folded flag in an unlabeled display case that only hinted at tragedy.

I also wondered if the Baker residence would

be as strange as Becca's since both moms were teachers. The Chapmans had no TV, healthy food in every cupboard, and a big mat by the entryway because visitors had to take off their shoes and pad around in sock feet.

Mrs. Baker's house was boringly normal. In fact, except for the large cardboard box with the sides trimmed to six inches sprawled across the laundry room floor, it looked too normal. Mom would be relieved.

I figured the cardboard box was the "whelping" box since it was lined with a couple of faded towels and an old baby blanket with a thrift store tag still attached. I'd looked up "whelping" in my school dictionary to discover it had to do with mammals giving birth.

Just like Poco, Pixie was at the door when I arrived. She didn't dance around, though, like Poco did. She paced slowly, like it was uncomfortable to move and just as uncomfortable to stop. Pixie was every bit as cute as Poco, so I didn't cut corners walking and petting her. Walking her, I discovered the back of the Bakers' was just a narrow alley away from the Wrangleys'. Unfortunately I couldn't use it as a shortcut on my bike because the passageway would be too tight of a squeeze for the handlebars.

It was now ten thirty. I supposed I could go home, shower, change, fix my hair, do makeup, and make it back closer to twelve thirty than noon, thus allowing plenty of time to meet Pete at school by two.

As my legs pumped the pedals on the way home, I revisited telling Mom about the date. But her words about a parent powwow that could result in a tightening up on my whereabouts spooked me. Maybe she'd forget the thought occurred to her. I decided to play it safe and keep quiet.

I really hoped she and Dad didn't have some talk about me being less free to come and go as I pleased. If they did, this dating thing could get real complicated.

CHAPTER 27

I was 99 percent sure this was a bona fide date and Pete was going to pay, but I brought the rest of the pet-sitting money I hadn't spent on the bike, just in case. Plus, I didn't want my dad to "accidentally" borrow it like he had the eighty dollars I'd slaved to earn for an *Oklahoma* costume.

I need not have bothered. Pete paid for everything, and I mean *everything*.

He insisted we get all kinds of snacks, saying in his best Texas Oil Man drawl that he'd recently come into some money. I felt terribly spoiled.

Until disaster struck.

A popcorn husk got stuck between two teeth. There is no graceful way to take care of that problem while sitting next to your boyfriend even if the movie theater is dark. It might have been my first date, but I knew digging around in my mouth like a dentist would not be attractive.

I excused myself to the restroom. A vaguely familiar skinny girl reapplying black lip gloss and eyeliner suggested using the rubber band I had tied my hair back with as floss.

Note to self: Never, ever go on a movie date without dental floss, because hair bands are too gross a substitute except in cases of dire emergencies.

When I slipped back into my seat, I realized Pete's arm was already on the back of it. If that didn't make it hard enough to concentrate on the movie, Pete reached with his other hand to hold mine. I wished for an Arctic blast to keep my hand from sweating since I'd ignored the advice of my coverless teen magazines.

It had recommended dusting your hands with cornstarch before a date, but I figured it would just wear off on my bike trek. I need not have worried. Every time a tense action scene of the SEALs saving somebody came on, Pete let go and cheered, giving me a chance to wipe my hand on my pants.

On screen, the Navy SEALs hunted terrorists, and I found some of my nervousness draining away as I got caught up in the excitement and tension on screen. As the final scene played out, I was relieved that not only had the United

States SEAL Team prevailed, but I hadn't done anything klutzy like spill popcorn all over or dump my soda in Pete's lap.

"Gabby," Pete whispered.

I turned. Pete's face was maybe two inches from mine. I nearly recoiled from the surprise of it, but his hand tightened on mine, and I suddenly got butterflies in the pit of my stomach.

Was Pete about to kiss me?

He closed his eyes. His face got closer and closer, lips mere millimeters from my own. I was pretty sure we were going to kiss, and I was terrified, thrilled, and totally unprepared.

I closed my eyes and hoped for the best. His lips touched mine. They were warm and drier than I expected. A lot drier than dog kisses.

Wow.

Sort of.

I mean, it was the first time I'd been kissed on the mouth by a boy that wasn't my brother or Mark Harrison from the second grade. It was pretty quick; at least I thought so, but with your eyes closed and your mouth covered by a boy's lips, you lose track of time. Those teen magazines ought to warn about that.

Then I realized my eyes were still closed, so I

opened them. Pete was looking at the screen, but I could tell he was smiling.

I wondered if I should have kissed him back. Or maybe I did but didn't know it.

Your first kiss was supposed to be all fireworks and swooning, right? A milestone on the adolescent expedition to adulthood. And I had no idea if I'd blown it or not.

CHAPTER 28

"Poco, you have it easy. Me, I've got big problems," I said as the tiny Chihuahua danced around my legs. "How come dogs can kiss anyone, anytime, and even if you have bad breath, you are totally unselfconscious about it?"

There was something absolutely unfair about the whole kissing thing. I was sure dogs didn't agonize about smooching so much they found themselves unable to talk afterwards.

I felt so awkward when Pete and I walked out of the movie that I had pretended I had to leave right away to pet sit. It wasn't until I was three blocks away that I realized I hadn't even thanked him or considered the possibility that Pete might feel like I took off because I didn't like the kiss. Or him.

To make matters worse, Amos jumped all over me for being thirty minutes early. I pondered investing the cash I hadn't needed at the movie for a watch. I inwardly giggled at the thought of asking Raff to recommend a good place to get one secondhand.

It was starting to lightly drizzle, so Poco and I jogged back to the Wrangleys'. I could hear Amos walking around upstairs and decided to get out before he had the chance to find fault with something else. I hopped on my bike, wishing I could take the shortcut through the tiny alley since I had dressed to impress, not to stay dry.

I tried to hurry into the Bakers' so the water running off of the roof over the side door didn't completely soak me. I hadn't noticed earlier that the gutters were in such bad shape. Of course, nobody notices gutters until they fail. Then it's too late. As I wiped my feet, I could hear Pixie whining.

Is she okay? Are the puppies coming? Are they here?

I felt a spark of excitement and glanced at her food bowl. The food was still untouched, and a puddle of what looked suspiciously like dog vomit was under the kitchen table. Pixie entered from the hallway, shivering and whining. She stopped halfway to me to pant like she'd just finished a marathon. She turned in a circle twice, then came and nosed my hand.

This isn't normal dog behavior. The puppies are coming!

Pixie started to squat, then paced a bit, and looked like she might squat again. I quickly clipped the lead onto her collar, opened the back door, and stepped into the storm. Cleaning up the vomit would be bad enough. There was no way I was going to clean up anything else.

I hoped Pixie would quickly do her business, especially since the drizzle seemed to be turning into a full-fledged downpour. The greyhound was in no hurry, unfortunately. I was turning up my collar when Pixie nearly jerked the leash from my hands.

I was not about to lose the leash. I grabbed it tightly with both hands. Bad move. Pixie twisted around to face me and then scooted backward.

In the process, she slipped her collar.

My heart rate increased.

This wasn't good. It wasn't good at all.

CHAPTER 29

I lunged to grab Pixie but stumbled in the wet grass. Pixie seized the opportunity and made a beeline for the shed. I chased after her.

I was too slow.

The back end of the pregnant animal disappeared under the toolshed.

I sloshed over, calling to Pixie. The shed looked like it was on its last legs—literally. The wood looked rotted and the roof patched. The front end was propped off the ground about eight to ten inches on crumbling cinder blocks, but the back end was not just touching the ground, it looked like it had sunk in.

I squatted down, rain plastering my red hair against my face. I had to brush it away to peer under the shed. I couldn't see much, but something moved around, and I heard whining.

"Come on, girl. That's no place to have puppies," I coaxed in my best syrupy sweet voice. "Let's go back into the nice, warm, dry house."

Instead of heeding my words of wisdom, Pixie stopped moving and might have lain down. It was too dark to tell. The rain was turning the bare earth spots into micro swamps. Cold water was sliding down my back where it had wormed its way under my collar.

The shed wasn't large, but if Pixie was dead center, I would have to lie flat to get ahold of her. That meant getting my date clothes slathered in mud. It was a disgusting thought.

Plus, what if she tries to bite?

Mrs. Baker had warned me that after the puppies came, Pixie might try to bite if I got too close. I wondered if that might apply before or during the whelping process. *Whelping* was going to go on my list of least favorite words ever.

The clouds unleashed their stuff, and I was thoroughly soaked. I decided to get a stick and try to gently poke her out. I couldn't find a stick, so I ran back inside to retrieve a broom or mop. I also grabbed a couple of dog biscuits and shoved them in my pocket, thinking maybe I could tempt her out with those. The food bowl seemed to laugh at my idea, but it was all I had.

The sky had darkened even more in that

fragment of time. I stared at the side of the shed, planning to sweep the mop handle from the back forward, to dislodge Pixie from her doggy spa. I tried the first time without really looking since I didn't want to kneel in mud, but squatting just didn't provide any leverage. I couldn't tell if her hole was so deep I'd passed over it, or if I was missing her entirely.

I bit the proverbial bullet and dropped to my knees. My pants had been pretty well soaked through, but I felt the squishy mud squirting from beneath me until my left knee painfully discovered a piece of crumbled brick.

Ouch!

I peered through the murk and gloom. I positioned my mop handle for another sweep when the shed shifted. The back end sank at least half an inch and pressed the mop handle into the ground. I had to jerk it to get it out.

Time for Plan B.

I lay flat in the mud. I called and coaxed. It rained harder.

I reached under as far as I could, holding out a biscuit. Pixie only whined in reply. The shed shifted again, getting dangerously close to my outstretched arm. I yanked it out.

I used my hands to shield my eyes and

looked carefully. The back end was definitely sinking. Maybe the dog had dug underneath it or maybe it was the derelict condition of the shed, but for whatever reason, the structure was sinking into the soft ground underneath it.

I'd have to crawl under and grab her. From the front, where there was the most space.

What if the shed slips further, trapping you like it almost did the mop handle?

My mind conjured up the unwelcome image of the Wicked Witch in *The Wizard of Oz*, boots sticking out from under Dorothy's house that had fallen on top of her and killed her. I shivered, only partly because of the cold and wet. I did not want to end up like the Witch.

Nobody will come looking for you until your mom gets home at 10:30. You'll be either crushed to death or drowned by then.

If you don't do something, Pixie and the puppies will drown or be smushed.

Call for help.

That just might work.

I gauged the distance the shed had sunk and figured I had three minutes to make a phone call.

In other words, I didn't have a second to spare.

CHAPTER 30

I raced inside, heedless of the mud I tracked in, and snatched the phone off the wall. I hurriedly dialed my house.

Please let my dad be home. Please let him answer.

After ten rings I hung up and tried Becca's. Even if we weren't exactly on speaking terms right now, she'd never let the pregnant Pixie and the puppies drown. Maybe her dad would come help me or at least tell me what to do.

But no one picked up. It went to the answering machine.

I slammed the phone down. Time was running out.

In desperation, I dialed one of the only other numbers I knew by heart—Pete's number. Lana answered on the fourth ring.

I had no time for pleasantries. "I have to talk to Pete. It's an emergency," I yelled.

Lightning flashed outside as the storm worsened.

"Sure . . ." Lana said in a teasing sort of voice.

I didn't have time for this. The rumbling thunder served to remind me of that. "Lana, I'm not kidding. It's about a dog in danger!"

I hoped she'd tap into her own feelings about when Fluff had disappeared and take me seriously. She did.

"Pete! Phone! It's Gabby."

I let out the breath I didn't know I was holding as Lana's voice became muted. I wanted to yell and tell her to stay on the line, not to leave me alone like this. I realized I was starting to panic and willed myself to stay calm, to breathe, to think.

"Gabby?" Pete's voice sounded surprised, hopeful, and confused all at once.

"Pete, listen. I need your help." I quickly gave him a rundown of the situation.

"Can you prop the shed up?" He sounded too tentative, too unsure.

"I don't think so. Help me. I don't know what to do."

"You need an adult."

"I know," I said desperately, staring at the back door. "But there aren't any available right now, and Pixie and the puppies . . ." I choked on the rest of the sentence.

"My parents are gone and Lana can't drive," Pete said in an earnest voice.

At least he'd grasped the seriousness of the situation, but I needed much more than that if Pixie and the pups were to survive.

"Gabby, hang tight. I'll ride my bike over. As fast as I can. Don't do anything dangerous 'til I get there."

"Okay," I said, wondering as it slipped out if I was telling the truth. I gave him the address and ended with "Hurry!"

I hung the phone up and rushed back outside. I dropped down, heedless of the cold mud. Rain was pouring down, and I couldn't be sure if Pixie was still under the shed.

The shed was still sinking, and time was running out.

I looked around for something to stick under the dilapidated structure, something that wouldn't sink into the mire.

Nothing.

I remembered hearing about a lady who lifted a Volkswagen off her husband when the jack holding it up collapsed, trapping him underneath. Something about adrenaline giving you superpowers. It was worth a try.

I took a wide stance, squatted like the

Russian weightlifters did, reached under the front of the shed, and tried to flip it over. My feet only sank deeper into the mire. Mud oozed over the tops of my dress boots.

Where are Russian weightlifters when you need them?

An idea as bright as lightning flashing above and just as fast zoomed through my mind.

The SEAL lifted weights. Huge weights. I bet he could bench a gazillion pounds.

My brainstorm gave birth to hope.

SEALs did all sorts of dangerous stuff.

They were heroes. They saved people. Amos could save Pixie!

Reality slammed down and burst the bubble of hope. My SEAL was a grouchy, disabled mess.

But, at the moment, he was all I had.

CHAPTER 31

If necessity was the mother of invention, desperation was the father of bravery. Sometimes you had to go with what you had.

I raced out of the yard, across the street, sideways through the narrow alley, and up the Wrangleys' steps in a time that would have earned me an A in PE for life. I banged on the door with one hand while I fished for the key ring in my pocket.

He was just here fifteen minutes ago. He never leaves. Please don't let this be the one time he ventured outside.

The door swung open just as my fingers closed on the keys. I nearly fell flat as I stumbled into the entryway. Amos stared at me like I was Looney Tunes, and only then did I think about what I must look like: a rain-soaked, muddy mess—maybe even like a homeless person.

The irony wasn't lost on me, but I had other, more important things to think about. Like what

I was going to say.

"There's a dog trapped under a shed. It's sinking into the mud. Going to have babies any minute now. Have to get the shed up. I need you to come." The words jumbled and tumbled together.

Amos continued to stare at me like I had escaped from Virginia Beach Psych. "You're dripping mud all over," he finally said.

I opened my mouth, ready to blast him about the insignificance of a little mud in the grand scheme of things, but I stopped myself in the nick of time.

"I'll clean it up. Later. Right now we have to save Pixie!" I gasped, still trying to catch my breath.

"What do you expect me to do?" He unfolded his arms and pointed at his bandaged leg. His face spoke volumes.

I might as well have requested that he fly to the moon and bring me back a cheeseburger.

"Please. The shed is sinking. I can't get my dad or anyone else. You were a SEAL. You used to save people. You can do . . . something!" I sucked in a shaky breath, on the verge of tears.

"Sorry, I can't help you." He pointed again at his leg and tapped his cane. As he turned away, he called over his shoulder. "Don't worry about the mud. I'll get it."

Time. There was no time. No time for this. Without thinking it through, I grabbed his arm and yanked. He wasn't expecting it. He whirled, and I saw something cold and akin to fury cross his face as he jerked free. I thought he might hit me. Then the fire bled out of his eyes and his gaze was merely stony.

Words jumped out of my mouth, like stampeding cattle. I was so red-hot mad I didn't try to stop them. "You could at least try. I'm going to. You'll feel like a real jerk when you find out I drowned or got crushed under the shed while you lay around feeling sorry for yourself."

The words might as well have been a hand slapping him across the face. Like runaway cattle, there was no calling them back. His eyes blazed again with an angry fire.

I didn't care. I glared back for two seconds, and then charged out the open door.

I leaped off the porch and prepared to dash back to the Bakers' when I heard him call after me.

"Not so fast! I don't know where this crisis is." He'd said the word "crisis" sarcastically, but

I didn't care. He was hobbling down the stairs, his flip-flops slapping the soles of his feet.

He was going to help, I realized.

Thank goodness, he was going to help.

CHAPTER 32

By the time we got to the shed, it had sunk enough that the front was only about four inches above the ground—not nearly enough space for Pixie to crawl out, even if she wanted to. The shed leaned to one side more than the other. Only the mop head was visible. The handle was completely buried.

Thunder rumbled in the distance, which I hoped meant the storm was blowing over. It might slow the sinking of my personal *Titanic*. I realized then that the rain was dropping rather than pounding on us.

We had a chance. We had to have a chance.

Amos jammed his cane under the shed and tried to lever it up. The cane snapped in two.

I dropped to the ground and tried to locate Pixie. Something moved under the shed, and I heard whining. Then she thrust her nose into my hands. Her front paws were next. Her head could only make it partway, confirming that she was too big to fit through the space left.

She had realized the danger too late. It was too late to crawl out. We were all just too late. Unless . . .

Unless all that iron pumping had given someone steel muscles. Unless adrenaline really could give you the strength to lift a car or a shed.

Amos squatted and grabbed the edge of the shed.

"I'm going to lift up. You pull."

I nodded. The shed started to rise, but his feet, especially the bad one, slid out from under him, and he tumbled to one knee with a grunt.

"Try again; this time brace my foot with yours," he commanded, pointing to the mud adjacent to his bad leg.

I did.

He grabbed and tried a second time. I concentrated on not letting my foot slip. It was no use. His good foot slid out from under him this time. Pixie yelped as the shed sank deeper into the mud.

"I need something to stand on, something with traction," he said through gritted teeth.

I nodded and made a beeline to the house, nearly flattening Pete as he came through the side gate. Our bodies collided, and we both fell.

I was on my feet in a heartbeat, but Pete just stared, stunned by the collision, my appearance, or probably both. The front of his beige rain jacket was now smeared with mud.

I grabbed his hand and helped haul him to his feet.

"Towels and the doormat." I whirled and yanked the door open.

Pete's feet squishing in the puddles behind me calmed me a fraction. I grabbed the towels out of Pixie's whelping bed and pointed to the doormat. Pete grabbed it and followed me.

"Who?" both guys said at the exact same time.

"Later," I yelled.

Amos snatched the towels and doormat from us and placed them under his feet. Pete took in the scene, his face a mixture of confusion and hopelessness. Pixie clawed at the mud, desperately trying to get out. I dropped down to pat her, then joined her efforts, scooping as much mud as I could from beneath the sinking shed.

"Stop! That will just make it worse. You!" Amos barked at Pete. "Stand here."

Pete complied.

"Brace my foot with yours, like this." Amos

demonstrated with his good leg, and then took a wider stance. "You!" He looked at me. "On the other side."

I scrambled to obey. Pixie's muzzle popped out right next to my foot. She must be sensing we were doing everything we could to save her.

But could we? Would we?

"On three, we all lift. Just a few inches. Just enough for her to crawl out. But we have to hold it until she's out."

We nodded. The sky had cleared enough to make Pixie's predicament plain. It was now or never.

"One, two, three!" Amos shouted.

We strained.

My fingernails dug into something soft and squishy on the underside of the shed, but I didn't care. My feet were trying to slide, but I refused to let them. The blankets provided just enough traction for my feet to stay put.

The shed seemed to shift imperceptibly. Maybe a millimeter at the most. Pixie moved. I felt her nose by my foot. Then the shed moved up another notch. I heard both of the others grunting and wondered if I was too.

Another millimeter and a sucking noise. The dog's head pressed against my foot as she clawed her way by digging into my ruined boots. The shed shifted up, but the boards underneath my hands started crumbling apart. I was losing my hold. Pixie's shoulder or flank passed my trembling leg.

My back strained. My arms shook. I tried to hold on, but the rotten wood was disintegrating. It was slipping from my grasp.

Then I felt rather than saw that Pixie was out.

The three of us let go, and I fell back, butt landing in a squishy piece of churned, sloppy ground. I didn't care. We'd done it. We'd saved Pixie!

She stood like a clay-covered statue, the sky sprinkling her enough to cause rivulets of dirty water to run off of her head, back, and tail.

Both Pete and Amos reached down to haul me up. The rain had turned to a fine mist that was gently washing the mud from the shivering dog's form. She was okay.

But could her puppies still be under there?

I hadn't realized I had said it aloud.

"No way," answered Amos. "A mother dog would have carried one out with her if there had been any, plus she'd be digging at the mud to get back there after the rest."

"Good to know," I mumbled.

He turned to Pete. "Good thing you showed up when you did." Amos clapped Pete on his back. "Without you, this mission would have failed."

Pixie gave an excited bark, and all three of us turned to see Mrs. Baker and Hannah, travel bags in hand, gaping at us in shock.

CHAPTER 33

"Amos Harper?" Mrs. Baker whispered.

"Cordelia Baker?" Amos looked dumbfounded.

Whoa! Mrs. Baker and Amos knew each other?

As their little reunion began in the sopping wet yard, Pixie in the center of their little circle, Pete and I looked at each other.

"Cordelia?" Pete whispered. His jacket and the Spiderman shirt underneath it were soaked. His pants were splattered with mud, shoes covered with glop. He glanced behind me as a car pulled to a stop. "I gotta go. My aunt's waiting."

I grabbed his hand and made him face me. "Pete, thanks for coming. Spiderman couldn't have saved the day any better than you did."

Pete looked at me, and then glanced quickly at his feet as he swiped a foot across a puddle. "The SEAL guy did all the lifting." He shrugged and pointed to Amos as he disappeared inside the house with Hannah and Mrs. Baker.

"Pete, you saved the day." I waited until he looked up. "We tried and failed before you got here. Amos has a bad leg. If you hadn't come when you did and braced his foot with yours, we'd have failed again and again until it was too late. You made all the difference."

He tapped the puddle a few times with his glop-coated tennies, then looked back up directly into my eyes. "Do you really think so?"

His face looked so very vulnerable I almost felt like crying. What I thought mattered, mattered in a most desperate sort of way. Never before had my opinion meant so much. I broke into a grin and grabbed his other hand.

"I know so." I wanted to hug him, make him feel my sincerity, wash away all the doubt and evict bad feelings that resided in his heart. The ones his parents had put there without meaning to.

Before I could reach for him, Pete had pulled me into an embrace. It started soft and tentative, then fierce. The next thing I knew, he'd pushed me away just enough so that his mouth could cover mine.

I forgot the rain, the cold, the mud covering both of us, and kissed him back.

This time I didn't worry about if I was doing it right. This time I meant it with all my heart. My whole body felt like it was submerged in warmth, like the sun was brushing me with its golden rays both inside and out.

We walked hand in hand to his aunt's car. I was relieved to see it wasn't brand new or anything. He got in but didn't close the door.

"Call me tonight, okay?" Pete said, looking at me intently. He was sitting tall and proud, smiling, not caring that he dripped gunk and looked like a pig farmer.

"Absolutely." I waved until the car turned the corner and disappeared out of sight. I was still feeling tingly warm and happy and brave and in control.

Then it hit me.

His aunt's gray car looked just like the car we'd chased yesterday.

CHAPTER 34

"What happened to you?" My dad looked confused and irritated as he stared at me.

I was covered in mud from hair to sock feet. I'd dumped my jacket and boots on the porch, trying to minimize the mess. Apparently I had failed, because dark rings spread out from my feet and soaked the welcome mat.

I launched into the story, but Dad waved me off and lumbered toward the TV room before I'd even gotten to the part where Pixie disappeared under the shed.

I hope Pete's parents are more appreciative.

Pete. My heart skipped a beat, and I grinned. But only for a second.

The gray car. My heart thudded into a pit swirling with questions, regret, and fear. Nausea crawled out of the pit and into my stomach.

All this ick is making me sick. I need to shower. I'll see this more clearly when I'm clean.

After tossing everything into the washer and

scrubbing in the shower, I pulled out Dr. Watson to try to sort through my conflicting thoughts.

I made columns, labeling them Pete, Raff, Paws and Furballs, and Pollack Labs.

Under Pete I wrote: blond hair, gray car, wants to be a hero, jealous of Lana, knew about dogs being boarded, new bike, money for movie, knew about ruby bracelet.

I hated the fact his list was so long. But Dr. Watson was insisting I write down the facts, and all of them.

Under Raff I wrote: new watch, history of criminal activity, knew about ruby bracelet (probably), pit bull, near gray car.

Under Paws and Furballs I wrote: needs money and wants publicity.

Under Pollack Labs I wrote: Hannah's papers, needs animals, truck at Animal Control.

I reviewed what I wrote, and my heart sank. Pete's list was still the longest.

I needed to confront him and get it over with. Ask about the gray car. Even though I'd seen someone else in a black sweatshirt get inside, that didn't mean that Pete couldn't be somehow involved.

I hunted for the phone. It wasn't on the charger or in my room or anywhere I usually left it. I finally tried the TV room. Dad was focused on the Hawaiian Surfing Championships flickering across the screen. The plastic antenna of the phone was peeking out from under the couch.

"Your mother and I went to these." My dad nodded toward the screen. "Right after we got married. A honeymoon business trip. I made it to the semifinals before the grandfather of all mondo waves wiped me out."

A smile played on his lips as he remembered his glory days, but I'd heard this story too many times to let it interrupt my pressing investigation.

I scooted the phone out and clicked "talk." Nothing happened. The battery was dead. I groaned inwardly. Since the phone was old and usually took hours to recharge when it was this dead, I'd have to call Pete in the morning.

***

Sunday morning I'd been home a solid hour after pet sitting Poco, wondering if 7:30 was too early to call Pete. I didn't know if Pete's family went to church or not. If they did, they might be up, but still be home.

My family didn't go to church anymore. Mom, Timmy, and I had a couple of times to some cathedral thing for Easter services and at Christmas before his disappearance. Right after Timmy vanished, people held a candlelight prayer service at the beachfront. Even strangers had prayed for my brother's return. It didn't happen. I figured if there was a God, He was too busy to notice common people like us. He was probably too overloaded with wars and third world starvation to be concerned about one lost kid.

As I picked up the phone, it rang.

"Gabby, this is Paulette. From school. A policeman brought Puddles home last night."

My eyes widened with surprise. "That's great."

"She even had her collar on, and Daddy was really, really surprised about that. We're getting her a plain one today."

"Good idea. I'm really happy for you and Puddles." I felt guilty I hadn't done more to help her.

"I have to go. See you Monday." She hung up before I could say goodbye.

I glanced at the clock: 7:45 a.m. I dialed Pete's number and hoped he'd understand about the phone being dead last night. I didn't want him to think I'd stood him up.

A young voice I didn't recognize answered.

"Can I talk to Pete?" I asked sweetly.

In the background I heard a male whisper, "Who is it?"

"Who is this?" the voice I guessed belonged to Suzy asked obediently.

"Gabby." I almost added, "Pete's girlfriend," but stopped myself.

"Gabby!" the little voice called.

The faint male voice answered, "Not here."

"He's not here. Bye." Click.

I sucked in my breath, a numb hand dropping the phone. The voice was faint, but I was 99.9 percent sure my boyfriend had just told his sister to lie to me.

A thousand reasons zoomed inside my head, each vying for attention. They whizzed around like crazed bumblebees, making me feel dizzy and unable to focus on just one. I wanted to run away from it all, but my body was immobilized by the crushing realization that after everything—the movie, saving Pixie, the kisses—my boyfriend didn't want to talk to me.

The last thing I wanted to do was hang around the house, wondering where I had blown this whole BF-GF thing. I needed to take my mind elsewhere.

Watson suggested checking out the pawnshop where I'd seen Raff.

Who was I to disagree with a talking diary?

CHAPTER 35

The street was even less lively on a Sunday morning than on a weekday afternoon. I guessed it was one of those creepy places that came alive after dark, the kind where people who lingered too long never returned home or were never heard from again. I had to hunt for a place to lock up my bike. There was no way I was leaving it unlocked in a place like this.

The inside of Paradise Pawn surprised me. I figured it would be a jumble of junk, kind of like the non-chain thrift stores were. Instead, it was well lit and well organized, and the man waiting on a customer at the jewelry counter could have passed for a salesman at the mall.

"As you can see, a diamond easily cuts glass. Most diamonds of less than gem quality wind up in manufacturing to cut metals and other hard substances. But fine diamonds like this belong in the light."

I wandered closer and caught sight of the

sales guy scratching a piece of glass with a gemstone bracelet. I edged closer.

"So I can tell if a diamond is real or not by seeing if it will scratch glass?" asked the customer.

"Yes and no," answered Sales Guy. "Cubic zirconia, a synthetic gem often substituted for diamonds, is hard enough to scratch glass and most metals. You'd have to be a pro like me to tell the difference. But if it's rhinestones, the other substitute for the real deal, you could tell. They're soft and don't cut glass."

I edged even closer. Sales Guy smiled at me and held the bracelet so I had an unobstructed view.

"An interesting tidbit of history here: Georges Frederic Strass invented the rhinestone in 1724, and his work was so admired that even King Louis XV of France ordered paste copies of his crown jewels. Back then they referred to rhinestones as paste jewels because they were made from a mixture of glass and lead."

A woman wearing a leopard-print dress and a ton of bling came from behind the stereo stuff to join us. "I think I saw a story on TV once about a lady who thought she'd lost an expensive bracelet she borrowed and bought a replacement only to find out years later, after she went broke paying for it, that she'd only lost a paste copy," she said.

"Yes, it was a necklace, though." Sales Guy was turning the charm up as his audience grew. "The show you saw must have been based on a short story called 'The Necklace.' But you are right about the rest. Rich people often have paste fakes made to wear in public so that if they ever got robbed, they really didn't."

Leopard Print smacked her gum and asked in a nasally voice, "If I brought in a picture of something one of the stars wore to the Oscars, could you make a rhinestone copy for me?"

"I can't, but I can arrange for it with guys who do it all the time. In fact, they can do next-day service for a few dollars more."

It hit me so suddenly I got goose bumps. Someone could have dropped off the collar to get a paste copy made. That would let them sell the real one and put a paste version on Puddles, and no one would be the wiser.

It was a real possibility.

"Can rubies cut glass?" I asked.

"Yes. They are almost as hard as diamonds. Funny you should ask, since someone was in here not long ago asking about paste rubies."

Bingo!

"For a dog collar?" I asked.

Sales Guy looked at me over the rim of his frameless glasses. All the friendliness had drained from his eyes, but the smile stayed on his face like toast crumbs that should be brushed away.

"No," he said a bit too firmly, like he was trying to convince me. He deliberately turned away and began a sales pitch to Leopard Print. "Let me show you the earrings that match this bracelet."

I didn't care. I was about to break this case wide open.

CHAPTER 36

As I pedaled home, I had it all figured out. Black Hoodie dropped off the collar to Sales Guy, who passed it on to the counterfeiters. They probably had a dingy underground lair where they manufactured the fakes. Raff was in on it, serving as a lookout when stolen jewels were brought in. And he stole the pit bull so he could sic him on anyone trying to rob the robbers.

I realized the last part sound pretty far fetched, but it was the only way I could tie in the other missing dogs. Plus, running scenarios through my head took my mind off Pete having his sister lie to me on the phone.

In my rush to call Paulette, I didn't bother taking off my jacket, which worked out since Paulette and her family were out (according to the maid who answered the phone) and Mom had other plans for me.

"Tootsie, the Wrangleys are home and need

their key back," she told me. "When you get back from returning it, we need to have a talk."

I could tell by her furrowed eyebrows that I was in hot water. Instead of trying to worm it out of her, I headed back out. Halfway there it hit me.

I forgot to clean up the mud!

The rest of the way I agonized on how to best apologize, but all my worry was for nothing. The Wrangleys thanked me and never mentioned the mud. As I took their key off my ring, I realized I still had Mrs. Baker's.

I headed right over and found my teacher carting plant pots and tools out of the shed. The structure slumped over like an old man with a bellyache.

"Hi, Mrs. Baker," I called out. "Sorry, I forgot to give this to you." I held out her key.

"Did Pixie have the puppies yet?"

She smiled. "All seven of them. Would you like to see them?"

"Absolutely." I followed Mrs. Baker inside.

Pixie rested on her side in the midst of seven of the cutest little greyhound puppies I had ever seen. Of course, they were the only greyhound puppies I had ever seen, but that was beside the point. Most of them were gray-brown like Pixie with white throats. The tiniest one was all brown except the tip of one ear. Another had a white throat and looked like he had kneesocks on his front feet and anklets on his hind paws.

I squatted down, careful not to get too close. Their little eyes were squeezed shut, but they rooted and burrowed with their pink noses, trying to find the warmest spot. They made tiny squeaky noises, especially when Pixie licked one of them.

"They're adorable," I said with a sigh.

"They are, aren't they," Mrs. Baker agreed. She was pulling cash out of her wallet.

"You don't need to pay me," I said.

Maybe that's what was up with Mom—she wanted to remind me not to take any money.

"Of course I do, Gabby. Without your quick thinking, they wouldn't be here."

"Please, my mom won't let me take any money. Really."

Mrs. Baker cocked her head to one side, then returned her money to her purse. "Who was that boy that helped you yesterday?"

"Pete—Lana's brother. He goes to our school, he just isn't an actor," I added.

"Give him my thanks. Amos told me how he couldn't have done it without him."

"I'll tell him. Can I ask you a question? For a friend, that is?"

"Sure, Gabby. Fire away." Mrs. Baker drew a chair in from the kitchen and sat. She must have guessed it was going to be a complicated question.

I sat on the floor. It might be a long answer.

"This friend of mine used to have just one friend, but now she has more friends and a boyfriend, and the first friend doesn't eat lunch with them anymore."

"I see. So what is the problem, exactly?" Mrs. Baker asked.

If I knew that, I wouldn't be here, I wanted to say. I didn't want to go into more detail either, or she'd know I was talking about myself. So I decided to try an economic angle.

"So in Civics—except it's the economics part right now—we're talking about opportunity cost and always having to give up the next-best thing to get the best thing, but I don't think it's necessarily true. I mean, can't you have both things? Both friends?"

It sounded a little confusing and stupid, so I hoped Mrs. Baker could sort it out. Most teachers were pretty good at that sort of thing, especially when you didn't want them to.

"People use the word 'friend' today to mean anything from a casual acquaintance to a longtime we've-gone-through-it-all-together best friend. I'm guessing the two original friends were more like the latter."

I was pretty sure *latter* meant the last one, so I nodded.

"It could be one friend is afraid of losing the other friend or that they won't be that close anymore," Mrs. Baker offered. "Usually same-gender friendships change once teens start dating. But girls seem to have the hardest time of adjusting their relationships, even if there is time for all friends."

"But why? It's not like a boy uses up all your friend-ness." I was pretty sure *friend-ness* wasn't a word, but I didn't know what the right word was.

"You might have the same amount of friend-ness, as you put it—at church we refer to that as *phileo* love, the friend kind of love. But with more friends, you have to divide your time and activities between them. I think that's where opportunity cost comes in." She paused and added, "It might be tempting for your friend to spend all her available time with her boyfriend, but it's probably smarter to balance things out.

Boyfriends come and go, but a good friend can stick closer than a brother."

"So, what should my friend do about her other friend?"

"Fear, especially fear of the unknown, can invite people to do things they normally wouldn't do. I would advise your friend to talk to her first friend about the whole situation. And I mean really talk, and as soon as possible. The longer things are wrong, the more likely they are to stay wrong."

That made sense. The longer Timmy was missing, the more Dad drank and the worse things got. But it wasn't fair or right because there was nothing I could do to fix it.

"Things don't always work out," I blurted, thinking of Timmy and Dad and even Mr. Baker's plane crashing.

"How do we know? We haven't come to the ends of our stories. Remember in *Oklahoma,* how everything looked dismal for Laurey, especially since Curly was on trial for killing Judd? Remember how the judge made it all work out?"

I nodded, easily recalling the details of the play that had been my stage debut.

"God is our judge. In the end, He'll set things to right, no matter how bad or unfair things seem or are right now. I find it comforting to know that in the scope of eternity, God has it all under control and everything will work out."

The doorbell rang. Mrs. Baker jumped up so quickly I thought she expected an invading horde of Martians to break down her door. A look of pure panic flashed across her features before she smoothed her dress and patted her hair. I noticed she wore makeup, which she never did at school. I'd been too engrossed with the puppies or my own problems to note that detail before.

Amos was at the door!

But instead of being dressed in sweats or like a bum, he had on nice slacks and a dress shirt. His hair was pulled into a ponytail, his beard and moustache trimmed and neat. He wore flip-flops, but the bandages were less bulky than before. He wasn't using a cane to walk, probably because he'd broken the only one he had saving Pixie. As he stepped inside I could see he limped, but a tiny bit, not like before.

Had saving the puppies changed him somehow? Or . . .

Mrs. Baker and Amos?

"I'm glad you decided to go to church with us this morning," Mrs. Baker said, welcoming him into her home.

Amos nodded, then spied me. He scowled for a fraction of a second.

Mrs. Baker turned to me and said, "Gabby, we have room for a fourth if you'd like to attend? Hannah will be down in a sec and would go with you to the youth group Bible study."

Behind her, upstage in theater talk, Amos was shaking his head and mouthing the words "you owe me" and "mud." He had a point.

"Thanks, but no thanks, Mrs. Baker. I have stuff I gotta do." *Like call the Zollins.*

"Okay, but know the invitation is always open," my teacher said with a sincere smile.

I didn't know what to say, so I softly called goodbye to Pixie and the pups and made a beeline for the back door, wondering what my mom wanted to talk to me about.

CHAPTER 37

"Gabby, your father and I are very disappointed in you." My mother uncrossed her arms and went back downstairs, leaving me to fume over the fact I was grounded.

Goth Girl had not just ratted me out for being at the movies with Pete, but she'd told my mom about the kiss as well. How was I supposed to know that my mom's thrift store friend was the same girl who'd been in the movie theater bathroom and suggested using my hair tie as dental floss?

I dialed the Zollins.

"Miss Paulette isn't here. Whom should I say called?"

"Gabby St. Claire," I said, forcing myself to speak sweetly and not scream. Since my whole life was pretty much shot, I figured I might as well call Becca and pile up my frustrations in one big heap.

"I suppose you called because you saw the

newscast and wanted to rub my face in it that I was wrong about Pete," Becca snarled.

I was taken aback. "No. I called . . . wait. What news story?"

"About the police busting up a major dogfighting ring, which was behind the kidnapping of the pit bull. The stupid criminals thought they could mislead the police by taking Fluff and the Irish setter, but police aren't that dumb, you know. They not only caught the dognapper, but busted everyone involved. But you can go ahead and gloat if you want."

"I don't want to gloat. I'm glad the police solved the case. Dogfighting is horrible. Was the pit bull okay and everything?"

"Yeah . . ." Becca's voice trailed off.

I waited.

When she spoke next, she sounded a smidgen less hostile. "The dogfighters had tried to buy or at least breed their dogs with Lucky—that's the pit bull. The owner suspected they were into fighting, so he kept refusing. He told the police about it, and with the help of Paws and Furballs, who'd already been trying to get some hard evidence against the creeps, they busted them."

"Becca, I didn't know anything about the

dogs or the police. I just called because I want whatever is wrong between us to be made right." There. I came out with it. Laid it on the line. Bared my soul.

I waited again.

"Oh," Becca said softly.

I could tell she was moving into another room because the sound of classical music in the background got fainter and fainter. I took it as a good sign that she was going for some privacy. Maybe we could patch things up. I heard a door close.

"So talk," she said, still a bit defensively.

"Why didn't you sit with us at lunch Friday?"

"I'm a fifth wheel."

"You're not. You're my best friend," I blurted. "I don't know what I did to make you so mad at me."

"For one thing, I'm not really mad at you. It's just that . . . well . . . life's not fair." Becca burst into tears.

For the next half hour she talked a little and cried a lot, but the long and short of it was, like Mrs. Baker kind of guessed, fear. Becca was afraid I wouldn't have time for her anymore. Or that I would dump her for Paulette because

Paulette had rich parents and Becca thought she had whack jobs. She was pretty bent at her parents because, even though she did everything right, except maybe that one B in math, they never let her do anything.

Anything she wanted, that was.

"So, what boy in his right mind, even when I am sixteen and even if I have straight As and whatever other impossible criteria my stupid parents throw in for good measure, what boy is ever going to come to the house and *meet my parents*?"

By *meet*, she meant get the third degree from her ex-marine cop father. I could totally see her point. You could be popular, fun, pretty, rich, and anything else that made the perfect girlfriend, but guys weren't going to be lined up so they could *meet* your monster father.

"I totally get why you didn't tell your parents," she said when I told her I was grounded and why.

"So Monday, you'll sit with us?" I asked.

"Of course, seahorse," she quipped.

"Becca, there is another thing." I filled her in about the Pollack Labs van at Animal Control, the gray car, and both trips to the pawnshop.

"Maybe Puddles is one of those copycat

crime things—someone taking advantage of the first crime to get away with a second, unrelated crime. I'll tell my dad when he gets home tonight."

I pulled out Watson and read her what I'd written under each suspect.

"I think we can eliminate Paws and Furballs," Becca said.

I agreed.

We mulled over each of the other three suspects and the evidence about each when my BFF said, "We have to ask: Who benefits if a ruby collar is missing?"

"Pollack Labs could use research animals," I suggested weakly.

"They aren't dumb enough to mess with the Zollins. Whoever took Puddles doesn't fully understand just how powerful the Zollins are."

"You're right." I drew a line through Pollack Labs.

"Raff has dark hair." Becca didn't want to say that. I could tell. But she was right.

That left only Pete on the suspect list. I wanted to explain to her all the reasons it couldn't be him, but before I could, she shouted into the phone.

"Just a second! I gotta go," she muttered.

"General Hitler just got home and is calling."

I bit back my disappointment. "Later, gator."

"See you at lunch, Cap'n Crunch."

"At noon, baboon."

Before I had time to let Pete's guilt sink in, the phone rang again. It was Paulette. I quickly explained my theory to her, but she couldn't seem to grasp what I needed her to do to test my hypothesis.

"Can you put your dad on the phone?" I finally asked.

I re-explained the whole ruby-scratching-glass thing to her dad, and in moments he confirmed what I had suspected.

The rubies were fakes.

I, Gabby St. Claire, am an amazing detective, just like Sherlock Holmes.

I told Mr. Zollin all about Paradise Pawn but left out the gray-car part. I knew I shouldn't have, but I just couldn't make myself mention it.

"Gabby, we appreciate this a great deal," her dad said. "Now I need you to keep a lid on this whole thing. I'll take it from here. Understand?"

"Yes, sir," I said reluctantly.

I doubted Mr. Zollin understood the irresistible urge to share my brilliance with the world. Or at least three thousand of my closest friends and acquaintances. It would be tough, but I'd manage. But at least I'd have the satisfaction of telling Becca, since she'd have to keep it quiet as well.

Paulette came back on the phone. "Gabby, next Saturday, would you come with Puddles and Mr. Jangles and me to get our pictures taken?"

"Sure," I said.

Then I remembered I was grounded.

CHAPTER 38

"Sh, here comes Brandon," Becca hissed.

I stopped midsentence. It was Friday, and all week Becca and I and even Paulette had kept a lid on the fake-collar news. It had almost been as torturous as being grounded and unable to spend time with Pete after school or to do something to prove him innocent.

Brandon plopped his lunch tray down. I craned my neck, looking for Pete in the knot of students exiting the lunch line.

"He's not coming," Brandon said, looking concerned.

"Why?" I asked.

"Lana said Pete is in big trouble." Brandon shrugged.

My heart froze.

Pete's been caught! Mr. Zollin took the fake collar to the police, who pulled off his fingerprints. Pete is in jail somewhere, and it's my fault!

"Isn't he in school?" I squeaked, hoping and

praying his parents had posted bail.

"No. Besides being grounded for life, they made an appointment for him with . . ."

"A lawyer?" I gulped.

"No," Brandon laughed. "Maybe a counselor. Or to get a shot."

As long as he's not getting shot.

"Parents overreact to everything," Becca ranted. "Last night my mom threw out all those magazines your mom gave us! She says I am not to read that 'trash' anymore. I need to focus on my studies—not boys, clothes, and 'trashy popular' music."

Paulette joined us, handing me a flyer about the Paws and Furballs fundraising photo shoot. I stuffed it in my pocket quickly, hoping to divert the conversation before Paulette could mention I was going with her Saturday. I worried Becca might pull back into her shell like a turtle surrounded by sharks. I mean, if it had been me, I would have seen Benedict Arnold written all over it.

"I'm glad you're going with me Saturday," Paulette said before I could choke down the peanut butter superglued to the roof of my mouth.

Even though I couldn't swallow in time,

Becca only arched her eyebrows and mouthed the word "grounded."

Grounded. Pete and I are both grounded. Did my mom call his parents?

As I pushed through the crowded halls after lunch, I tried not to worry about Pete. Instead I attempted to formulate a good argument to get me ungrounded by Saturday. I'd always wanted to ride horses either as a cowgirl rodeo star or possibly Lady Diana style. I even begged my parents to get me a free pony after reading *Misty of Chincoteague* and realizing that the ponies lived on an island not far from Virginia Beach. My parents said no to the pony, but Dad had promised to take Timmy and me to see the annual pony swim and auction on Pony Penning Day.

Once a year in July, saltwater cowboys swim some of the wild herd from the island to the mainland. Dad even promised we could watch from the water, perched on his surfboard.

Then Timmy disappeared, and so did all of Dad's promises. I'd outgrown the desire to have my own pony, but I would never outgrow the desire to have my little brother and my old dad back.

Lost in my own thoughts, I nearly ran over

Wanda and the Diva, chitchatting in the doorway of the Civics classroom. Wanda had wormed her way into the Cool Clique in record time. The whole group now wore matching necklaces, apparently ones they'd made at that sleepover.

I took my seat, and Mr. Cicorelli started passing back our quizzes from Thursday. I scowled at my red 73 percent until I saw the big, fat 71 percent the Diva had scored.

"Since everyone's quiz grades were low, I thought we'd better review and then retake the quiz," Mr. C. started. "Scarcity means we all have to make what?"

"Choices," shouted an eager kid in the front.

"Raise your hands and I'll call on you," Mr. C. said and continued slogging through the most boring stuff ever. "We all have to make choices, and choosing involves costs. Because of scarcity, you make choices, which means you give up the next-best alternative—the opportunity cost. Who can give me an example of an opportunity cost?"

He turned to face the class. Hands shot up all over.

"Food," someone said.

Mr. C. wrote it on the board under the word "needs."

Another student volunteered "video games," and our teacher wrote it under "wants."

I had a pretty good idea what was going on, so I raised my hand so Mr. C. would think I had been paying attention all along. With all those hands waving, I was pretty sure the odds were in my favor to not get called on.

"Donabell?"

"While for most people the photo shoot would be a want, for me it is a need because I'm going to be a professional actress and maybe model," she finished, striking what I imagined she thought of as her "brilliant student pose," and I wanted to gag. It worked on the teacher. Mr. C. smiled and nodded, the glare from the overhead lighting glinting off his balding head.

"Good point. Needs and wants are different for different people. How much in dollars will the photos cost?"

"Nothing. Wanda's paying for me. One regular and two costume poses." The Diva struck her I-am-a-star pose, chin in the palm of her hand.

I pulled the flyer from my pocket. The basic package cost a hundred dollars for three poses in your own outfit and a CD with one pose of the photographer's choice. But for each additional fifty dollars, you could get three poses in one of the period costumes that would be available.

My mouth dropped open. While I was no math whiz, I could tell this was way expensive. I worked it out. 100 + 50 + 50 = 200. Two people meant the total package was costing $400. My mom made about that much after putting in a forty-hour week at the drugstore. I was sure doctors like the Diva's dad made much more, but I could hardly believe people would drop that much on pictures of her on a horse.

You probably could buy a horse for $400!

A chilling question struck me. What if the criminals were planning on kidnapping more pets? I mean, Becca implied the police knew pets were being held for ransom, and someone had targeted Paulette and her family before. What if they realized how loaded they were and decided to strike again? Or maybe they wanted to get several pets at once like they did at Oceanside. This fundraiser would be the perfect place to do it.

I couldn't let that happen. Nothing and no one would disappear on my watch ever again.

As long as I could talk my parents into letting me go.

CHAPTER 39

Talking my mom into it had been easier than I thought. I'd promised to help her clean some houses as part of my punishment, and I'd reminded her that this was a once-in-a-lifetime opportunity. It probably helped that my dad was in a lousy mood and had fussed at me for leaving my shoes on the porch, so my mom had felt sorry for me.

While that had gone more smoothly than I ever imagined, trying to wash out the product I'd globbed into my hair, hoping to tame it, was not. The serum took out the frizz, all right, making my red tresses look like a matted, greasy mess.

Time was running out. The Zollins would be here to pick me up any minute now, and I wasn't wild about the shirt I'd picked out either. It was new, as in new to me, but I thought it made me look fat.

My mom had picked it up at Thrift World to

replace my best green sweater top that got ruined saving Pixie. She said the emerald green would accentuate my hair in a positive way. Which it might, but the banded bottom tended to ride up, making the lower half of the shirt poof at my waist, therefore making me look fat.

I also wondered if she had gone to Thrift World for another reason: checking in with Goth Girl the Spy. Not that I could really blame her. I should have talked to her about Pete and the movies.

"Gabby. They're here," my mom called upstairs.

I groaned. My hair was still damp. I didn't have time to blow-dry it or find a different shirt. I hurried downstairs, grabbed my jacket, and refused the toast my mom was holding out. No way was I going to get crumbs all over me and the Zollins' Rolls-Royce.

"At least drink this milk," my mom insisted.

I chugged it down, hoping I wouldn't burp in the car. I already perspired a little, nervous about being in unfamiliar territory and way out of my comfort zone. As I hustled to the gleaming navy vehicle, I reminded myself today wasn't about me. It was about keeping Paulette and her pets safe.

A man I didn't recognize was driving. I wondered if he was a relative or a chauffeur. As I scooted in the back beside Paulette, I checked out her outfit. Black, almost knee-high boots covered the lower half of her beige, close-fitting riding pants. Her black show jacket looked expertly cut and tailored, with three gold buttons and two front pockets. Peeking out at the neck was a brilliantly white high-collared shirt. Her riding helmet was on the seat beside her, and her ruby tennis bracelet sparkled on her wrist.

I probably looked like a scullery maid.

"I took your advice and left Puddles at home. It would be fun to have pictures of her and me on Mr. Jangles, but it is more important she's safe." Paulette smiled at me with a simple, childlike expression as I buckled up.

The scent of her floral cologne tickled my nose, and I wondered if she only wore it on weekends or if the fragrance got lost in a sea of adolescent hormones at school.

"Daddy signed you up too. I figured you wouldn't be afraid to get on a horse. I could see you riding western, doing barrels or poles. I'd be afraid of banging my knees into the poles, but you aren't afraid of anything."

I conjured up an image of someone doing limbo on horseback. "I'm cool with horses. Thanks. You didn't have to do that, you know."

"I wanted to, and the money goes to a good cause. I'm just glad you're not afraid of big animals or anything."

No, I wasn't afraid of horses or doing poles, whatever that was. I was afraid of different things, much different things. One of which was messing up. Either from not knowing social protocol at such a ritzy place or by failing as a bodyguard.

Gabby, chillax! No Puddles means no dognapping. The worst thing that can happen is stepping in manure.

I forced myself to settle into the soft leather upholstery and enjoy the thirty-minute ride. But I couldn't shake the feeling something was going to go terribly wrong.

CHAPTER 40

I imagined Beach Barn and Riding Academy as a red barn surrounded by acres of grass and a white fence. I got the fence part right but was totally unprepared for three ginormous barns, a lighted outdoor ring, and a jumping area. Signs pointed to trailheads that disappeared into the wooded area surrounding one side of the complex. The other side and back were pastureland with horses grazing in the morning sunshine.

A girl could get used to coming to a place like this.

The barns or stables were heated and as clean as our house. They smelled of leather and freshly cut lawns. I spun in a circle as I followed Paulette, drinking in the sights, sounds, and smells.

Sawdust muffled our footsteps inside the larger stable, but the sounds of horses snorting, tack jingling, and mounted riders surrounded us. We headed over to the area next to the women's locker room, where a photographer and his white umbrella thingies were set up. He was snapping away at the most beautiful horse and rider I had ever seen.

"Wow," Paulette whispered. "She looks like she stepped out of Camelot or someplace."

"Unlike some people."

I turned my head in the direction of the Diva's all-too-familiar voice.

"This event is for charity, not charity cases."

She gave my outfit a cold once-over, and I self-consciously tugged the poufy shirt down. Wanda, standing next to her, had the good manners to at least look embarrassed.

A tall, thin man with gold-rimmed glasses and a clipboard approached. "Miss Zollin. So glad you could make it."

At that precise moment, the sorrel lifted his tail and relieved himself. Immediately, a stable hand wearing a black T with "Beach Barns—the next best thing this side of heaven" emblazoned on it stopped brushing the Shetland pony, grabbed a shovel and whisk broom, and scooped the poop. He handed it off to a blond-haired kid, also in jeans and black T, who headed away from us.

Whoa! That kid looks familiar. Very familiar.

Pete!

What was Pete doing here?

I tried to duck around the Diva to catch a better look at his retreating figure, but she chose that exact moment to put her hands on her hips and step into my path. I twisted awkwardly to avoid bumping her. By the time I looked again, the guy had vanished.

"I want the golden horse." The Diva enunciated each word. "Do whatever you have to do to make it happen."

The Diva snapped her fingers in the poor man's face before turning on her heel and marching off to the women's locker room.

I rolled my eyes. The Diva was a legend in her own mind. Wanda looked bewildered, like she couldn't decide if she should follow the Diva or flee. After a moment's hesitation, she followed.

"You two go ahead and change while I round up your Mr. Jangles," a relieved Mr. Clipboard said. Reluctantly, I headed after the Diva, but before ducking inside, I scanned the area once more, trying to catch a glimpse of Pete or his body double.

Why would Pete be here? How did he get

here?

I checked out the rack of clothes and chose a blue calico dress that reminded me of my costume for *Oklahoma*. Paulette couldn't decide between cowgirl and Plains Indian outfits.

While I waited, I tried to decide if I'd really seen Pete. The more I thought about it, the more ridiculous I realized the idea was. Neither he nor Lana rode horses, so he had no reason to be here. He couldn't drive, and it wasn't likely he'd cycled out here, starting at sunrise or before, because he was grounded.

I sighed. It was wishful thinking.

Wanda appeared, probably tired of the Diva by now. She nodded at my selection, then checked out Paulette's choices.

"This one," she said, pointing to the cowgirl option. "But your tennis bracelet isn't period. It will ruin a great look. I can hold it for you." She held out her hand.

I bristled. Wanda seemed a bit too eager. Besides, if anyone was going to hold a gazillion-dollar piece of jewelry, it would be me, the bodyguard.

"I got this," I said, all but yanking the bracelet out of Paulette's hand before Wanda could touch it. I stuffed it deep into my back jeans pocket.

Wanda smiled at me, and I felt ashamed.

I, Gabby St. Claire, jump to conclusions way too easily.

"Forget the hat," Wanda counseled when Paulette picked one up. "You don't want to cover such beautiful hair."

"What about my hair?" snapped the Diva, obviously displeased to see Wanda talking to us. She shot flaming arrows from her narrowed eyes. Wanda cringed, and a hint of a smile tugged at the corner of the Diva's lips.

I glared back, wishing my eyes shot laser beams that could erase that smug look off her face. I hoped Wanda was having second thoughts about trying so hard to fit with the Cool Kids.

"Come on, Paulette," I said, heading toward a stall. "Let's change."

CHAPTER 41

I managed to mount Mr. Jangles without falling off or ending up facing backward. I tugged the waistband of the shirt down and smoothed the poufy part out. Giving the photographer my best Kate Moss smile, I sat up straight in the saddle.

Click.

"Look a bit towards your right," he instructed.

As I turned, I caught a glimpse of someone with blond hair just like Pete's ducking down behind a stall. My mouth dropped open.

Click.

"Try to keep your mouth closed," the photographer instructed.

I complied, deciding that as soon as my shoot was done, I'd have to find that kid and determine once and for all if it was Pete.

"Stop scowling."

Click.

Gabby! Focus. This is a once-in-a-lifetime opportunity. Mr. C. mouthing "opportunity cost" flooded my mind as I realized I had to choose between good pictures or getting to the bottom of a mystery. It was not a choice I wanted to make.

"Hold that look!"

Click.

"Nice. Very studious."

Click.

Out of the corner of my eye, I saw Wanda, hat pulled down over her face like a disguise, moving away from the cluster of watchers. She seemed to be scanning the people around her, almost slinking into the locker room.

Maybe she's going to ditch the Diva.

Click.

I wondered whose parents had driven them here. I knew the Diva's parents' cars all too well from the time my mom and I had cleaned out their garage. I didn't think I saw either of those, and I didn't know what Wanda's folks drove.

But I did. I remembered back to that rainy day when she'd come to school with orange hair. They had a gray car. A gray car just like the one I'd seen near the pawnshop.

Click.

She'd dyed her hair blonde after the Diva had made fun of the orange. Blonde like what was under the ski mask when Puddles was dognapped.

She had enough money to pay for new clothes and this photo shoot.

She'd sat with us the day Becca snapped at Paulette about the ruby collar and tennis bracelet.

The tennis bracelet! It was in my pants! In the locker room! Where she was headed.

Click!

I ducked under Mr. Jangles and vaulted over the fence. I collided with a woman exiting the locker room. I landed on my butt, but before I could think to say "sorry," I saw Wanda ducking into the stall where I'd changed. I scrambled up.

I squeezed around the woman I'd knocked into just as Wanda, exiting my stall, saw me. Panic crossed her face, and something sparkled in her hands. She spun and headed the opposite way, toward the showers.

I had her trapped.

CHAPTER 42

Only she wasn't trapped.

On the other side of the showers was another door, and Wanda disappeared through it. I followed, struggling to run in a long dress, and burst into a small arena.

Wanda looked right and left. Something was clenched in her right fist. She drew that fist back like she was preparing to pitch a softball.

She'd ditch the bracelet rather than be caught, I realized.

I had to catch her before she tossed the bracelet. There would be no evidence. The bracelet would be lost.

And I, Gabby St. Claire, would look like the biggest bozo in the world.

"Stop her! She's a thief!" I yelled before thinking it through.

What if I was wrong? It would be the most humiliating time in my life, even worse than the time I got kicked out of the cast of *Oklahoma.*

Just then, a stableboy dove out of a stall and tackled her. The two of them tumbled to the floor, disturbing horses and riders. Wanda squirmed out of his grasp, but I managed to dodge a kid and his pony to pin her legs down.

"It's in her right hand. Get it," I demanded.

The guy complied, easily wresting the jeweled bracelet out of her unclenched hand.

I got my first good look at the guy who tackled her, my deputy.

He wasn't a stable hand.

He was Pete.

"What?" I started to say, but Wanda was crying and speaking at the same time.

"I'm sorry. I'm sorry. I didn't want to do it. But he said I had to or he'd hurt my mom!" Wanda blubbered like a preschooler. "I told him about the ruby collar, and this was his idea. I tried to talk him out of it!"

A stern-looking woman wearing a riding academy polo shirt and carrying a riding crop glared down at us. I rolled off Wanda and swallowed, wondering if this severe-looking woman might whack us with her crop.

"You better have a good explanation for endangering everyone in the vicinity with your behavior," she barked, tapping the crop against her tall black boot.

"She stole an expensive ruby bracelet." I nearly choked on the words. "From my friend, Paulette Zollin."

Those seemed to be magic words, as her eyebrows shot up.

"She's already confessed. Here it is." Pete held the bracelet high.

Wanda was huddled into a tight ball, her sobs shaking her whole body. She was blubbering something about doggies or Doug in a tiny, frightened voice.

"Take them to my office while I call the police," Riding Crop said to another staff member.

Pete grabbed my free hand in his. When he squeezed, I felt like he'd transferred some sort of superhero steel into my blood. It would be all right.

I, Gabby St. Claire, had this situation under control.

EPILOGUE

"So your parents had you see a shrink?" Becca asked.

"A counselor. They thought I made the whole Pixie thing up to get out of trouble for muddying up my aunt's car. And because they also thought I was obsessive compulsive or something about finding Fluff, they had me talk to this guy," Pete explained over lunch the next Monday.

"Did you have to lie down on a couch?" asked Paulette.

"No," Pete said with a laugh, "but I sure told him how I felt about Lana being the center of their universe. But the best part was seeing their faces when they found out what happened at the stable and that I really had saved Pixie."

Pete grinned ear to ear, shoulders thrown back, his chest puffed out to make Superman, or at least the Superman T he wore, proud.

"Actually, Gabby was the one who figured

everything out," said Paulette sincerely.

One glance at Pete's crestfallen face and I knew that was absolutely the last thing Paulette should have said. Even if it was mostly true.

"It does no good to figure things out if you don't have the muscle to make things happen." I smiled at Pete, hoping he'd buy it. "Plus there's the timing. Pete responded faster than a speeding bullet both times I needed him. A minute later would have been too late."

It did the trick. Pete puffed back out and stayed that way even when Brandon laughed, "Wasn't there enough manure at the stables? You have to bring it here?"

Everyone but Paulette laughed.

"They don't. They clean it up and give it away as fertilizer," she said sincerely.

No one bothered to explain the joke to her, but they didn't laugh at her either. We were all back to accepting each other as we were and enjoying each other's company in the chaotic Oceanside cafeteria.

Wanda had confessed to dognapping Puddles at the insistence of her mother's druggie-criminal boyfriend, Dougie. He'd frightened her into being his partner in crime.

Becca's dad had filled in the blanks. Wanda's

mom had met the creep in drug rehab in the western part of the state. Dougie had moved back to Virginia Beach with them and convinced Wanda that her mom would somehow suffer unless Wanda did exactly what he told her to. He wanted Wanda to get in with the wealthier crowd so she would have access to their homes and could case them before he burglarized them.

Mr. Chapman said Wanda had wanted to get caught and Doug the Thug, as I called him, was awaiting trial. My BF's dad told us the Pollack Lab van at Animal Control was just a guy picking up his runaway pet.

The best thing he'd told me was "good job." Since it was coming from a police officer, I took it as the highest form of praise. I just wished he hadn't lectured us about stranger dangers like we were six-year-olds for another hour and a half.

"Why is it so hard for parents to believe the best about their teenage kids?" Pete asked. "Why was it so unbelievable that I could be a hero?"

"Parents! They think because they brought you into this world, they are allowed to make you wish they'd take you out," Becca groused.

Everyone chuckled, but I knew Becca wasn't joking. She was changing, morphing out of the obedient little caterpillar into something else. I just didn't know what.

But I, Gabby St. Claire, would get to the bottom of that mystery, too.

"Yeah, but sometimes making you miserable backfires," Pete said with a big grin.

To punish him for getting his aunt's car all muddy, they had made him "volunteer" to clean out the stables at Beach Barn, where his aunt worked weekends as a cashier. Pete was too embarrassed to tell any of us, but I had to give him credit for making lemonade out of a lemon when he decided to take photos of me during his Saturday stint.

The ones he'd given me turned out great. Even if the professional ones Paulette's parents were paying for were technically better, they'd never mean as much to me as his did. His were from the heart.

I thought maybe I'd drop by Mrs. Baker's and thank her for helping "my friend" unsnarl the tangled mess with her BFF. And maybe she and I could sort out some opportunity-cost stuff that baffled Watson and me.

Like, how did Wanda get in a situation where the opportunity cost for keeping her mom safe was doing something illegal? And if she had refused to go along with Dougie's plan and her mom got hurt, how could she live with that? How does someone like Wanda, or even me, keep from being in a position where you have to choose between two bad choices?

I, Gabby St. Claire, still had some personal mysteries to solve.

###

QUESTIONS

- When Gabby's brother vanished, people prayed for his return. It didn't happen, so Gabby figured if there was a God, He was too overloaded with wars and third world starvation to be concerned about one lost kid. Do you agree or disagree? (Read Matthew 18:11–14, Matthew 10:29–31, and Luke 12:6–7 before making up your mind.)

- Pete doesn't like being the middle child. Where are you in the birth order of your family? Does it make a difference? How or why? Is it best to be firstborn? Last? Middle? An only? How can parents treat their children the same while still respecting their individual differences?

- Hannah gets upset about using animals in research. Should companies test products on animals? Why or why not?

- Gabby sometimes wishes conversations came with a rewind button. Have you ever wished you could push the rewind button on a conversation? When and why?

- Gabby and Mrs. Baker talk about life not being fair. Mrs. Baker takes comfort in knowing that in the scope of eternity, God has it all under control and will set things right, no matter how bad or unfair things seem or are right now. Read Romans 8:28, Matthew 6:34, Joshua 1:9, and Jeremiah 29:11. Do these scriptures support or contradict what she believes?

- Gabby accepts a part-time job as a pet sitter. What qualities would you want in a person taking care of your pets? If you were going to have a part-time job, what would it be?

- Gabby gets in tight spots while pet sitting and wishes she could phone for help. If you were in a tight spot, who would you call and why?

- Mrs. Baker quotes Proverbs 18:24: "There is a friend who stays closer than a brother." What qualities are necessary for a close friendship like that? If someone doesn't have those traits, what can they do to develop them?

- Opportunity cost is defined as the next-best alternative not chosen, or the alternative given up, when we make a decision. What are some recent decisions you have made, and what were their opportunity costs?

- Sometimes Gabby feels like she is swimming upstream or being pushed along like an old bottle in the ocean. Do you ever feel that way? What advice would you give her?

- How old or mature should people be before they begin to date? How can someone tell if they are ready? Who should decide: parents, teens, or both?

- Mrs. Baker tells Gabby that same-gender friendships usually change once teens start dating and girls seem to have a harder time adjusting their relationships. How can friends work through these changes as they occur?

- If you had been Wanda, what would you have done? Why? If Wanda had asked you for advice, what would you have told her?

- For more discussion questions and a free novel study packet for *The Disappearing Dog Dilemma*, visit TeachersPayTeachers. http://www.teacherspayteachers.com/items/edit/1143069

About the Authors:

Kathy Applebee:

Kathy Applebee is an author, playwright and Virginia's 2011 Middle School Science Teacher of the Year (according to the Virginia Association of Science Teachers). She is a frequent contributor to PLAYS, the Drama Magazine for Young People and Fools For Christ. When she's not writing, teaching or directing plays, she can be seen on various stages in Virginia Beach, Virginia. Her favorite roles to date include the Wicked Witch of the West, Ouiser (Steel Magnolias) and Lady Macbeth.

Christy Barritt:

USA Today has called Christy Barritt's books "scary, funny, passionate, and quirky." Christy writes both mystery and romantic suspense novels that are clean with underlying messages of faith. Her books have won the Daphne du Maurier Award for Excellence in Suspense and Mystery, have been twice nominated for the Romantic Times' Reviewers' Choice Award, and have finaled for both a Carol Award and Foreword Magazine's Book of the Year. She's married to her Prince Charming, a man who thinks she's hilarious—but only when she's not trying to be. Christy's a self-proclaimed klutz, an avid music lover who's known for spontaneously bursting into song, and a road trip aficionado. For more information, visit her website at: www.christybarritt.com.

Sneak Peak!

THE BUNGLED BIKE BURGLARIES

(The Gabby St. Claire Diaries, Book 3)

By Christy Barritt and Kathy Applebee

CHAPTER 1

"Shakes on eight!" Mrs. Baker shouted.

Forty Oceanside Middle School thespians began shaking their limbs one at a time to a count of eight. To any outsider, we might have looked like spastic morons. But to insiders, this was a traditional warm up that helped prepare us for walking the boards—theater talk for being on stage.

I loved theater, the butterflies and all. The only thing that could make drama club better: having my boyfriend Pete next to me instead of resident diva Donabell Bullock.

That's right. I, Gabby St. Claire, had managed to stay in a romantic relationship for roughly one month, two days and about three hours, give or take five minutes. Not that I was counting or anything.

"Vocal warm ups! Unique New York."

Obediently, we all began speaking the words, slowly and quietly at first, building to a loud, fast staccato rhythm. At least, in theory we did. Most everyone messed up after the fifth or sixth time. It was a tough three-word combo, and I was determined to be the first one who'd do it seven times fast without faltering.

In the distance, I spotted an electrician wearing gray coveralls with "Zollin Industries" on the back disappear backstage. A moment later he appeared on the catwalk, an elevated platform above us that spanned the width of the stage and gave tekkies access to the gel-covered stage lights. Only half of the lights were on right now, probably because of the work being done in one corner.

"Take a seat." Mrs. Baker's voice managed to be loud and soft at the same time.

One day, when I was on Broadway, I'd be able to speak like that.

"As you know, I was able to convince the administration to allow us to do one more play this year. However . . ."

Uh oh. Howevers are never good when it comes to the powers that be at school. My BFF Becca and I exchanged glances. Her pixie haircut matched her pixie nose but contrasted sharply with the long legs she had folded underneath her.

I would have traded my frizzy red hair for

her dark brown on-its-best-behavior-every-day hair in a heartbeat. I would have gladly borrowed a couple of inches as well to add to my short five foot two frame. But just two. I wanted to stay shorter than Pete.

Not that Pete had ever said anything about not liking tall girls. But he did resist my encouragement for him to try out acting today. A sharp elbow in my ribs made me jerk back to the present.

"So, you will choose a character from a novel or a real life person with a connection to one of your classes," Mrs. Baker said, "and write your own monologue from their POV."

The Diva's hand shot up.

"POV as in point of view or the perspective of one particular character?" The Diva (the private code name Becca and I had assigned the snooty Donabell Bullock back in fifth grade) glanced around with an air of superiority.

"That is correct," Mrs. Baker said. "All the teachers, except a couple, are on board with this counting as an extra credit assignment."

Extra credit was good, especially if it concerned my math grade. But knowing my pre-algebra teacher Ms. Lynnet, the worst math teacher in the entire world, I'd bet dollars to donuts she was one of the "couple" who didn't want to co-operate.

Becca raised her hand. "If the person we choose overlaps two subjects, can we submit the piece to both teachers?"

Leave it to overachieving Becca to ask a question like that. But since her parents had pulled her out of our previous production of *Oklahoma* for one lousy B in pre-algebra, I figured she was just trying to milk this monologue thing for all the academic credit she could get to appease her overly strict parents.

"That's between you and them. Did you have someone in mind?"

"George Washington Carver, Thomas Jefferson, or Alexander Graham Bell. They are scientists and historic."

"They're male. You can't play a male character." The Diva scowled at my BFF, probably upset she hadn't thought of it first.

A glance at Becca's crestfallen face launched me into action.

"She could play one of their female relatives," I shot back, wishing I could actually, physically hit her between the eyes with one of those suction-tipped arrows. It would stick to her forehead, making her look ridiculous for once. The mental image made me grin. She locked her Frosty the Snowman eyes on mine and wrinkled her too long nose in distaste.

"Right you are, Gabby," said Mrs. Baker.

I basked in her praise as the Diva's death ray stare grew twenty degrees colder.

"Please turn your rough drafts into me *before* a week from Friday. If your monologue is chosen, you will have first dibs on performing it."

"Mrs. Baker." Brandon Coe's arm went up. "If I chose a famous dancer, can I incorporate dance into the monologue?"

"Absolutely." Mrs. Baker's smile and eyes beamed.

She became increasingly enthusiastic as we got more jazzed up about this whole thing. I just wished I hadn't daydreamed during the majority of her talk. But Becca would have all the details when we talked on the phone tonight. I could count on her to pay attention and fill me in.

The remainder of our meeting flew by as we played theater games and did improvisation exercises. I loved improv. It was one of the few times that acting first and thinking it through later could actually be a virtue.

"Call me before eight," Becca reminded me

as she dashed out the door after practice.

My reply got lost under the front row of seats. My backpack had tipped over spilling its contents. It was tough to find everything in the darkness, but no way did I want to feel around on the cold, sloping floor and encounter stuff like ABC (already been chewed) gum, dead roaches or whatever other horrors might lurk in an ancient school almost half a century old.

"Take a look at this."

The deep, unfamiliar male voice surprised me and, in my haste to see who was talking, I banged the back of my head on the underside of a seat. A few strands of hair stuck. I tugged it free realizing with a lurch in my stomach I had ABC gum attached to my already disastrous hair.

Yuck!

The voice had come from high on the ladder. The electrician was holding something about the size of a textbook, only round. "Some kid must have stuck this up in the eaves when the place was being built," said Deep Male Voice.

"What is it?" asked Mr. Harold, one of the OMS janitors.

"Dunno. The lid's rusted on. Probably junk. Might as well trash it."

I, Gabby St. Claire, was the next Sherlock Holmes, a solver of mysteries. No way was I going to let them trash whatever it was until I got a good look at it.

"Can I have it?" I called as I shrugged into my backpack and trotted backstage.

Visions of opening it and discovering pirate booty or a map to buried treasure filled my head. I saw myself being a teenage millionaire. I'd buy one of those big homes on the beach at Sandbridge. Mom could quit work and we'd drive a Rolls Royce like the Zollins.

Or maybe it would contain some secret science stuff, hidden away until a future age was ready to receive it. I'd be interviewed on talk shows and give speeches about my discovery. A professional hair and makeup expert would with travel with me so my fly away red hair would finally settle down and look fabulous. By the time I'd been on every TV station in the country, I'd be as famous as Sherlock Holmes.

"Here you go, Gabby," said Mr. Harold, depositing the grubby cylinder into my hands.

I sneezed. I could feel rather than see the rust underneath the coating of dust. I figured if it was as valuable as I thought it was, I'd better not open in front of adults. They just might decide to take it back and I'd lose out on the silver doubloons or crown jewels or secret spy messages it contained.

"Thanks, Mr. Harold."

"Take it home and squirt some WD-40 on it," suggested the custodian.

"WD-40?"

"Lubricating oil. Your dad probably has some in your garage. It does wonders on rusty things like bike chains."

"Thanks." I didn't add that my father had nothing but old surfing equipment and rusting tools in the garage. Or that he rarely did anything except sit on the couch. But if WD-40 had to do with bikes, Pete might be able to help me out. Pete took better care of his new mountain bike than most people took care of their kids.

I tried stuffing it in my backpack, but I needed more room. I slipped my civics book out and hid it under a seat then hurried out to the bike rack, eager to delve into another mystery, one that would make me rich and famous.

When I stepped outside, I froze when I spotted a patrol car and police officer next to my bike.